The Weird Menace Collection

By

Robert Ervin Howard

Contents

Black Talons

Black Talons... 3

Moon of Zambebwei

Chapter 1. The Horror in the Pines 21

Chapter 2. Black Torture... 25

Chapter 3. The Black Priest 30

Chapter 4. The Black God's Hunger 37

Chapter 5. The Voice of Zemba................................. 44

Skull Face

Chapter 1. The Face in the Mist................................. 53

Chapter 2. The Hashish Slave 55

Chapter 3. The Master of Doom 58

Chapter 4. The Spider and the Fly 61

Chapter 5. The Man on the Couch 66

Chapter 6. The Dream Girl 70

Chapter 7. The Man of the Skull............................... 72

Chapter 8. Black Wisdom 75

Chapter 9. Kathulos of Egypt................................... 78

Chapter 10. The Dark House.................................... 83

Chapter 11. Four Thirty-Four................................... 90

Chapter 12. The Stroke of Five 92

Chapter 13. The Blind Beggar Who Rode 96

Chapter 14. The Black Empire.................................. 98

Chapter 15. The Mark of the Tulwar 106

Chapter 16. The Mummy Who Laughed 110

Chapter 17. The Dead Man from the Sea................. 114

Chapter 18. The Grip of the Scorpion..................... 120

Chapter 19. Dark Fury.. 127

Chapter 20. Ancient Horror.................................... 132

Chapter 21. *The Breaking of the Chain/* 140

Black Wind Blowing

Chapter I - "I Take This Woman!"........................... 149

Chapter II - "Tell Them--In Pity's Name"................ 156

Chapter III - Dead Madness 160

Chapter IV - Crackling Blue Flame 166

Black Talons

Black Talons

Joel Brill slapped shut the book he had been scanning, and gave vent to his dissatisfaction in language more appropriate for the deck of a whaling ship than for the library of the exclusive Corinthian Club. Buckley, seated in an alcove nearby, grinned quietly. Buckley looked more like a college professor than a detective, and perhaps it was less because of a studious nature than a desire to play the part he looked, that caused him to loaf around the library of the Corinthian.

"It must be something unusual to drag you out of your lair at this time of the day," he remarked. "This is the first time I ever saw you in the evening. I thought you spent your evenings secluded in your rooms, pouring over musty tomes in the interests of that museum you're connected with."

"I do, ordinarily." Brill looked as little like a scientist as Buckley looked like a dick. He was squarely built, with thick shoulders and the jaw and fists of a prizefighter; low browed, with a mane of tousled black hair contrasting with his cold blue eyes.

"You've been shoving your nose into books here since six o'clock," asserted Buckley.

"I've been trying to get some information for the directors of the museum," answered Brill. "Look!" He pointed an accusing finger at the rows of lavishly bound volumes. "Books till it would sicken a dog--and not a blasted one can tell me the reason for a certain ceremonial dance practiced by a certain tribe on the West African Coast."

"A lot of the members have knocked around a bit," suggested Buckley. "Why not ask them?"

"I'm going to." Brill took down a phone from its hook.

"There's John Galt--" began Buckley.

"Too hard to locate. He flits about like a mosquito with the St. Vitus. I'll try Jim Reynolds." He twirled the dial.

"Thought you'd done some exploring in the tropics yourself," remarked Buckley.

"Not worthy of the name. I hung around that God-forsaken Hell hole of the West African Coast for a few months until I came down with malaria--Hello!"

A suave voice, too perfectly accented, came along the wire.

"Oh, is that you, Yut Wuen? I want to speak to Mr. Reynolds."

Polite surprise tinged the meticulous tone.

"Why, Mr. Reynolds went out in response to your call an hour ago, Mr. Brill."

"What's that?" demanded Brill. "Went where?"

"Why, surely you remember, Mr. Brill." A faint uneasiness seemed to edge the Chinaman's voice. "At about nine o'clock you called, and I answered the phone. You said you wished to speak to Mr. Reynolds. Mr. Reynolds talked to you, then told me to have his car brought around to the side entrance. He said that you had requested him to meet you at the cottage on White Lake shore."

"Nonsense!" exclaimed Brill. "This is the first time I've phoned Reynolds for weeks! You've mistaken somebody else for me."

There was no reply, but a polite stubbornness seemed to flow over the wire. Brill replaced the phone and turned to Buckley, who was leaning forward with aroused interest.

"Something fishy here," scowled Brill. "Yut Wuen, Jim's Chinese servant, said *I* called, an hour ago, and Jim went out to meet me. Buckley, you've been here all evening. *Did* I call up anybody? I'm so infernally absent-minded--"

"No, you didn't," emphatically answered the detective. "I've been sitting right here close to the phone ever since six o'clock. Nobody's used it. And you haven't left the library during that time. I'm so accustomed to spying on people, I do it unconsciously."

"Well, say," said Brill, uneasily, "suppose you and I drive over to White Lake. If this is a joke, Jim may be over there waiting for me to show up."

As the city lights fell behind them, and houses gave way to clumps of trees and bushes, velvet black in the star-light, Buckley said: "Do you think Yut Wuen made a mistake?"

"What else could it be?" answered Brill, irritably.

"Somebody might have been playing a joke, as you suggested. Why should anybody impersonate you to Reynolds?"

4

"How should I know? But I'm about the only acquaintance he'd bestir himself for, at this time of night. He's reserved, suspicious of people. Hasn't many friends. I happen to be one of the few."

"Something of a traveler, isn't he?"

"There's no corner of the world with which he isn't familiar."

"How'd he make his money?" Buckley asked, abruptly.

"I've never asked him. But he has plenty of it."

The clumps on each side of the road grew denser, and scattered pinpoints of light that marked isolated farm houses faded out behind them. The road tilted gradually as they climbed higher and higher into the wild hill region which, an hour's drive from the city, locked the broad crystalline sheet of silver that men called White Lake. Now ahead of them a glint shivered among the trees, and topping a wooded crest, they saw the lake spread out below them, reflecting the stars in myriad flecks of silver. The road meandered along the curving shore.

"Where's Reynolds' lodge?" inquired Buckley.

Brill pointed. "See that thick clump of shadows, within a few yards of the water's edge? It's the only cottage on this side of the lake. The others are three or four miles away. None of them occupied, this time of the year. There's a car drawn up in front of the cottage."

"No light in the shack," grunted Buckley, pulling up beside the long low roadster that stood before the narrow stoop. The building reared dark and silent before them, blocked against the rippling silver sheen behind it.

"Hey, Jim!" called Brill. "Jim Reynolds!"

No answer. Only a vague echo shuddering down from the blackly wooded hills.

"Devil of a place at night," muttered Buckley, peering at the dense shadows that bordered the lake. "We might be a thousand miles from civilization."

Brill slid out of the car. "Reynolds must be here--unless he's gone for a midnight boat ride."

Their steps echoed loudly and emptily on the tiny stoop. Brill banged the door and shouted. Somewhere back in the woods a night bird lifted a drowsy note. There was no other answer.

Buckley shook the door. It was locked from the inside.

"I don't like this," he growled. "Car in front of the cottage--door locked on the inside--nobody answering it. I believe I'll break the door in--"

"No need." Brill fumbled in his pocket. "I'll use my key."

5

"How comes it you have a key to Reynolds' shack?" demanded Buckley.

"It was his own idea. I spent some time with him up here last summer, and he insisted on giving me a key, so I could use the cottage any time I wanted to. Turn on your flash, will you? I can't find the lock. All right, I've got it. Hey, Jim! Are you here?"

Buckley's flash played over chairs and card tables, coming to rest on a closed door in the opposite wall. They entered and Buckley heard Brill fumbling about with an arm elevated. A faint click followed and Brill swore.

"The juice is off. There's a line running out from town to supply the cottage owners with electricity, but it must be dead. As long as we're in here, let's go through the house. Reynolds may be sleeping somewhere--"

He broke off with a sharp intake of breath. Buckley had opened the door that led to the bedroom. His flash played on the interior--on a broken chair, a smashed table--a crumpled shape that lay in the midst of a dark widening pool.

"Good God, it's Reynolds!"

Buckley's gun glinted in his hand as he played the flash around the room, sifting the shadows for lurking shapes of menace; it rested on a bolted rear door; rested longer on an open window, the screen of which hung in tatters.

"We've got to have more light," he grunted. "Where's the switch? Maybe a fuse has blown."

"Outside, near that window." Stumblingly Brill led the way out of the house and around to the window. Buckley flashed his light, grunted.

"The switch has been pulled!" He pushed it back in place, and light flooded the cottage. The light streaming through the windows seemed to emphasize the blackness of the whispering woods around them. Buckley glared into the shadows, seemed to shiver. Brill had not spoken; he shook as with ague.

Back in the house they bent over the man who lay in the middle of the red-splashed floor.

Jim Reynolds had been a stocky, strongly built man of middle age. His skin was brown and weather-beaten, hinting of tropic suns. His features were masked with blood; his head lolled back, disclosing an awful wound beneath his chin.

"His throat's been cut!" stammered Brill. Buckley shook his head.

"Not cut--torn. Good God, it looks like a big cat had ripped him."

6

The whole throat had literally been torn out; muscles, arteries, windpipe and the great jugular vein had been severed; the bones of the vertebrae showed beneath.

"He's so bloody I wouldn't have recognized him," muttered the detective. "How did you know him so quickly? The instant we saw him, you cried out that it was Reynolds."

"I recognized his garments and his build," answered the other. "But what in God's name killed him?"

Buckley straightened and looked about. "Where does that door lead to?"

"To the kitchen; but it's locked on this side."

"And the outer door of the front room was locked on the inside," muttered Buckley. "Doesn't take a genius to see how the murderer got in--and he--or *it*--went out the same way."

"What do you mean, *it*?"

"Does that look like the work of a human being?" Buckley pointed to the dead man's mangled throat. Brill winced.

"I've seen black boys mauled by the big cats on the West Coast--"

"And whatever tore Reynolds' gullet out, tore that window screen. It wasn't cut with a knife."

"Do you suppose a panther from the hills--" began Brill.

"A panther smart enough to throw the electric switch before he slid through the window?" scoffed Buckley.

"We don't know the killer threw the switch."

"Was Reynolds fooling around in the dark, then? No; when I pushed the switch back in place, the light came on in here. That shows it had been on; the button hadn't been pushed back. Whoever killed Reynolds had a reason for wanting to work in the dark. Maybe this was it!" The detective indicated, with a square-shod toe, a stubby chunk of blue steel that lay not far from the body.

"From what I hear about Reynolds, he was quick enough on the trigger." Buckley slipped on a glove, carefully lifted the revolver, and scanned the chamber. His gaze, roving about the room again, halted at the window, and with a single long stride, he reached it and bent over the sill.

"One shot's been fired from this gun. The bullet's in the window sill. At least, one bullet is, and it's logical to suppose it's the one from the empty chamber of Reynolds' gun. Here's the way I reconstruct the crime: *something* sneaked up to the shack, threw the switch, and came busting through the window. Reynolds shot once in the dark and missed, and then the killer got in his work. I'll take this gun to head-quarters; don't expect to find any fingerprints except Reynolds', however. We'll examine the light switch, too, though maybe my dumb pawing erased any fingerprints that might have been there. Say, it's a good thing you have an iron-clad alibi."

Brill started violently. "What the Hell do you mean?"

"Why, there's the Chinaman to swear you called Reynolds to his death."

"Why the devil should I do such a thing?" hotly demanded the scientist.

"Well," answered Buckley, "I know you were in the library of the club all evening. That's an unshakable alibi--I suppose."

Brill was tired as he locked the door of his garage and turned to-ward the house which rose dark and silent among the trees. He found himself wishing that his sister, with whom he was staying, had not left town for the weekend with her husband and children. Dark empty houses were vaguely repellent to him after the happenings of the night before.

He sighed wearily as he trudged toward the house, under the dense shadows of the trees that lined the driveway. It had been a morbid, and harrying day. Tag ends of thoughts and worries flitted through his mind. Uneasily he remembered Buckley's cryptic remark: "Either Yut Wuen is lying about that telephone call, or--" The detective had left the sentence unfinished, casting a glance at Brill that was as inscruta-ble as his speech. Nobody believed the Chinaman was deliberately lying. His devotion to his master was well known--a devotion shared by the other servants of the dead man. Police suspicion had failed to connect them in any way with the crime. Apparently none of them had left Reynolds' town house during the day or the night of the murder. Nor had the murder-cottage given up any clues. No tracks had been found on the hard earth, no fingerprints on the gun other than the dead man's nor any except Buckley's on the light switch. If Buckley had had any luck in trying to trace the mysterious phone call, he had not di-vulged anything.

Brill remembered, with a twinge of nervousness, the way in which they had looked at him, those inscrutable Orientals. Their features had been immobile, but in their dark eyes had gleamed suspicion and a threat. He had seen it in the eyes of Yut Wuen, the stocky yellow man; of Ali, the Egyptian, a lean, sinewy statue of bronze; of Jugra Singh, the tall, broad shouldered, turbaned Sikh. They had not spoken their thoughts; but their eyes had followed him, hot and burning, like beasts of prey.

Brill turned from the meandering driveway to cut across the lawn. As he passed under the black shadow of the trees, something sudden, clinging and smothering, enveloped his head, and steely arms locked fiercely about him. His reaction was as instinctive and violent as that of a trapped leopard. He exploded into a galvanized burst of frantic action, a bucking heave that tore the stifling cloak from his head, and freed his arms from the arms that pinioned him. But another pair of arms hung like grim Fate to his legs, and figures surged in on him from the darkness. He could not tell the nature of his assailants; they were like denser, moving shadows in the blackness.

Staggering, fighting for balance, he lashed out blindly, felt the jolt of a solid hit shoot up his arm, and saw one of the shadows sway and pitch backward. His other arm was caught in a savage grasp and twisted up behind his back so violently that he felt as if the tendons were being ripped from their roots. Hot breath hissed in his ear, and bending his head forward, he jerked it backward again with all the power of his thick neck muscles. He felt the back of his skull crash into something softer--a man's face. There was a groan, and the crippling grip on his imprisoned arm relaxed. With a desperate wrench he tore away, but the arms that clung to his legs tripped him. He pitched headlong, spreading his arms to break his fall, and even before his fingers touched the ground, something exploded in his brain, showering a suddenly starless night of blackness with red sparks that were engulfed abruptly in formless oblivion.

Joel Brill's first conscious thought was that he was being tossed about in an open boat on a stormy sea. Then as his dazed mind cleared, be realized that he was lying in an automobile which was speeding along an uneven road. His head throbbed; he was bound hand and foot, and blanketed in some kind of a cloak. He could see nothing; could hear nothing but the purr of the racing motor. Bewilderment clouded his mind as be sought for a clue to the identity of the kidnappers. Then a sudden suspicion brought out the cold sweat on his skin.

The car lurched to a halt. Powerful hands lifted him, cloak and all, and he felt himself being carried over a short stretch of level ground, and apparently up a step or so. A key grated in a lock, a door rasped on its hinges. Those carrying him advanced; there was a click, and light shone through the folds of the cloth over Brill's head. He felt himself being lowered onto what felt like a bed. Then the cloth was ripped away, and he blinked in the glare of the light. A cold premonitory shudder passed over him.

He was lying on the bed in the room in which James Reynolds had died. And about him stood, arms folded, three grim and silent shapes: Yut Wuen, Ali the Egyptian, and Jugra Singh. There was dried blood on the Chinaman's yellow face, and his lip was cut. A dark blue bruise showed on Jugra Singh's jaw.

"The *sahib* awakes," said the Sikh, in his perfect English.

"What the devil's the idea, Jugra?" demanded Brill, trying to struggle to a sitting posture. "What do you mean by this? Take these ropes off me--" His voice trailed away, a shaky resonance of futility as he read the meaning in the hot dark eyes that regarded him.

"In this room our master met his doom," said Ali.

"*You* called him forth," said Yut Wuen.

"But I didn't!" raged Brill, jerking wildly at the cords which cut into his flesh. "Damn it, I knew nothing about it!"

"Your voice came over the wire and our master followed it to his death," said Jugra Singh.

A panic of helplessness swept over Joel Brill. He felt like a man beating at an insurmountable wall--the wall of inexorable Oriental fatalism, of conviction unchangeable. If even Buckley believed that somehow he, Joel Brill, was connected with Reynolds' death, how was he to convince these immutable Orientals? He fought down an impulse to hysteria.

"The detective, Buckley, was with me all evening," he said, in a voice unnatural from his efforts at control. "He has told you that he did not see me touch a phone; nor did I leave his sight. I could not have killed my friend, your master, because while he was being killed, I was either in the library of the Corinthian Club, or driving from there with Buckley."

"How it was done, we do not know," answered the Sikh, tranquilly. "The ways of the *sahibs* are beyond us. But we *know* that somehow, in some manner, you caused our master's death. And we have brought you here to expiate your crime."

"You mean to murder me?" demanded Brill, his flesh crawling.

"If a *sahib* judge sentenced you, and a *sahib* hangman dropped you through a black trap, white men would call it execution. So it is execution we work upon you, not murder."

Brill opened his mouth, then closed it, realizing the utter futility of argument. The whole affair was like a fantastic nightmare from which he would presently awaken.

Ali came forward with something, the sight of which shook Brill with a nameless foreboding. It was a wire cage, in which a great gaunt rat squealed and bit at the wires. Yut Wuen laid upon a card table a copper bowl, furnished with a slot on each side of the rim, to one of which was made fast a long leather strap. Brill turned suddenly sick.

"These are the tools of execution, *sahib*," said Jugra Singh, somberly. "That bowl shall be laid on your naked belly, the strap drawn about your body and made fast so that the bowl shall not slip. Inside the bowl the rat will be imprisoned. He is ravenous with hunger, wild with fear and rage. For a while he will only run about the bowl, treading on your flesh. But with irons hot from the fire, we shall gradually heat the bowl, until, driven by pain, the rat begins to gnaw his way *out*. He can not gnaw through copper; he can gnaw through flesh--through flesh and muscles and intestines and bones, *sahib*."

Brill wet his lips three times before he found voice to speak.

"You'll hang for this!" he gasped, in a voice he did not himself recognize.

"If it be the will of Allah," assented Ali calmly. "This is your fate; what ours is, no man can say. It is the will of Allah that you die with a rat in your bowels. If it is Allah's will, we shall die on the gallows. Only Allah knows."

Brill made no reply. Some vestige of pride still remained to him. He set his jaw hard, feeling that if he opened his mouth to speak, to reason, to argue, he would collapse into shameful shrieks and entreaties. One was useless as the other, against the abysmal fatalism of the Orient.

Ali set the cage with its grisly Occupant on the table beside the copper bowl--without warning the light went out.

In the darkness Brill's heart began to pound suffocatingly. The Orientals stood still, patiently, expecting the light to come on again. But Brill instinctively felt that the stage was set for some drama darker and more hideous than that which menaced him. Silence reigned; somewhere off in the woods a night bird lifted a drowsy note. There was a faint scratching sound, somewhere--

"The electric torch," muttered a ghostly voice which Brill recognized as Jugra Singh's. "I laid it on the card table. Wait!"

11

He heard the Sikh fumbling in the dark; but he was watching the window, a square of dim, star-flecked sky blocked out of blackness. And as Brill watched, he saw something dark and bulky rear up in that square. Etched against the stars he saw a misshapen head, vague monstrous shoulders.

A scream sounded from inside the room, the crash of a wildly thrown missile. On the instant there was a scrambling sound, and the object blotted out the square of starlight, then vanished from it. *It was inside the room.*

Brill, lying frozen in his cords, heard all Hell and bedlam break loose in that dark room. Screams, shouts, strident cries of agony mingled with the smashing of furniture, the impact of blows, and a hideous, worrying, tearing sound that made Brill's flesh crawl. Once the battling pack staggered past the window, but Brill made out only a dim writhing of limbs, the pale glint of steel, and the terrible blaze of a pair of eyes he knew belonged to none of his three captors.

Somewhere a man was moaning horribly, his gasps growing weaker and weaker. There was a last convulsion of movement, the groaning impact of a heavy body; then the starlight in the window was for an instant blotted out again, and silence reigned once more in the cottage on the lake shore; silence broken only by the death gasps in the dark, and the labored panting of a wounded man.

Brill heard some one stumbling and floundering in the darkness, and it was from this one that the racking, panting was emanating. A circle of light flashed on, and in it Brill saw the blood-smeared face of Jugra Singh.

The light wandered erratically away, dancing crazily about the walls. Brill heard the Sikh blundering across the room, moving like a drunken man, or like one wounded unto death. The flash shone full in the scientist's face, blinding him. Fingers tugged awkwardly at his cords, a knife edge was dragged across them, slicing skin as well as hemp.

Jugra Singh sank to the floor. The flash thumped beside him and went out. Brill groped for him, found his shoulder. The cloth was soaked with what Brill knew was blood.

"You spoke truth, *sahib*," the Sikh whispered. "How the call came in the likeness of your voice, I do not know. But I know, now, what slew Reynolds, *sahib*. After all these years--but they never forget, though the broad sea lies between. Beware! The fiend may return. The gold--the gold was cursed--I told Reynolds, *sahib*--had he heeded me, he--"

A sudden welling of blood drowned the laboring voice. Under Brill's hand the great body stiffened and twisted in a brief convulsion, then went limp.

Groping on the floor, the scientist failed to find the flashlight. He groped along the wall, found the switch and flooded the cottage with light.

Turning back into the room, a stifled cry escaped his lips.

Jugra Singh lay slumped near the bed; huddled in a corner was Yut Wuen, his yellow hands, palms upturned, limp on the floor at his sides; Ali sprawled face down in the middle of the room. All three were dead. Throats, breasts and bellies were slashed to ribbons; their garments were in strips, and among the rags hung bloody tatters of flesh. Yut Wuen had been disemboweled, and the gaping wounds of the others were like those of sheep after a mountain lion has ranged through the fold.

A blackjack still stuck in Yut Wuen's belt. Ali's dead hand clutched a knife, but it was unstained. Death had struck them before they could use their weapons. But on the floor near Jugra Singh lay a great curved dagger, and it was red to the hilt. Bloody stains led across the floor and up over the window sill. Brill found the flash, snapped it on, and leaned out the window, playing the white beam on the ground outside. Dark, irregular splotches showed, leading off toward the dense woods.

With the flash in one hand and the Sikh's knife in the other, Brill followed those stains. At the edge of the trees he came upon a track, and the short hairs lifted on his scalp. A foot, planted in a pool of blood, had limned its imprint in crimson on the hard loam. And the foot, bare and splay, was that of a human.

That print upset vague theories of a feline or anthropoid killer, stirred nebulous thoughts at the back of his mind--dim and awful race memories of semi-human ghouls, of werewolves who walked like men and slew like beasts.

A low groan brought him to a halt, his flesh crawling. Under the black trees in the silence, that sound was pregnant with grisly probabilities. Gripping the knife firmly, he flashed the beam ahead of him. The thin light wavered, then focused on a black heap that was not part of the forest.

Brill bent over the figure and stood transfixed, transported back across the years and across the world to another wilder, grimmer woodland.

It was a naked black man that lay at his feet, his glassy eyes reflecting the waning light. His legs were short, bowed and gnarled, his arms long, his shoulders abnormally broad, his shaven head set plump between them without visible neck. That head was hideously malformed; the forehead projected almost into a peek, while the back of the skull was unnaturally flattened. White paint banded face, shoulders and breast. But it was at the creature's fingers which Brill looked longest. At first glance they seemed monstrously deformed. Then he saw that those hands were furnished with long curving steel hooks, sharp-pointed, and keen-edged on the concave side. To each finger one of these barbarous weapons was made fast, and those fingers, like the hooks clotted and smeared with blood, twitched exactly as the talons of a leopard twitch.

A light step brought him round. His dimming light played on a tall figure, and Brill mumbled: "John Galt!" in no great surprise. He was so numbed by bewilderment that the strangeness of the man's presence did not occur to him.

"What in God's name is this?" demanded the tall explorer, taking the light from Brill's hand and directing it on the mangled shape. "What in Heaven's name is that?"

"A black nightmare from Africa!" Brill found his tongue at last, and speech came in a rush. "An Egbo! A leopard man! I learned of them when I was on the West Coast. He belongs to a native cult which worships the leopard. They take a male infant and subject his head to pressure, to make it deformed; and he is brought up to believe that the spirit of a leopard inhabits his body. He does the bidding of the cult's head, which mainly consists of executing the enemies of the cult. He is, in effect, a human leopard!"

"What's he doing here?" demanded Galt, in seeming incredulity.

"God knows. But he must have been the thing that killed Reynolds. He killed Reynolds' three servants tonight--would have killed me, too, I suppose, but Jugra Singh wounded him, and he evidently dragged himself away like a wild beast to die in the jungle--"

Galt seemed curiously uninterested in Brill's stammering narrative.

"Sure he's dead?" he muttered, bending closer to flash the light into the hideous face. The illumination was dim; the battery was swiftly burning out.

As Brill was about to speak, the painted face was briefly convulsed. The glazed eyes gleamed as with a last surge of life. A clawed hand stirred, lifted feebly up toward Galt. A few gutturals seeped through the blubbery lips; the fingers writhed weakly, slipped from the iron talons, which the black man lifted, as if trying to hand them to Galt. Then he shuddered, sank back and lay still. He had been stabbed under the heart, and only a beast-like vitality had carried him so far.

Galt straightened and faced Brill, turning the light on him. A beat of silence cut between them, in which the atmosphere was electric with tension.

"You understand the Ekoi dialect?" It was more an assertion than a question.

Brill's heart was pounding, a new bewilderment vying with a rising wrath. "Yes," he answered shortly.

"What did that fool say?" softly asked Galt.

Brill set his teeth and stubbornly took the plunge reason cried out against. "He said," he replied between his teeth, "'Master, take my tools to the tribe, and tell them of our vengeance; they will give you what I promised you.'"

Even as he ground out the words, his powerful body crouched, his nerves taut for the grapple. But before he could move, the black muzzle of an automatic trained on his belly.

"Too bad you had to understand that death-bed confession, Brill," said Galt, coolly. "I don't want to kill you. I've kept blood off *my* hands so far through this affair. Listen, you're a poor man, like most scientists--how'd you consider cutting in on a fortune? Wouldn't that be preferable to getting a slug through your guts and being planted alongside those yellow-bellied stiffs down in Reynolds' shack for them to get the blame?"

"No man wants to die," answered Brill, his gaze fixed on the light in Galt's hand--the glow which was rapidly turning redder and dimmer.

"Good!" snapped Galt. "I'll give you the low down. Reynolds got his money in the Kameroons--stole gold from the Ekoi, which they had stored in the ju-ju hut; he killed a priest of the Egbo cult in getting away. Jugra Singh was with him. But they didn't get all the gold. And after that the Ekoi took good care to guard it so nobody could steal what was left.

"I knew this fellow, Guja, when I was in Africa. I was after the Ekoi gold then, but I never had a chance to locate it. I met Guja a few months ago, again. He'd been exiled from his tribe for some crime, had wandered to the Coast and been picked up with some more natives who were brought to America for exhibition in the World's Fair.

"Guja was mad to get back to his people, and he spilled the whole story of the gold. Told me that if he could kill Reynolds, his tribe

15

would forgive him. He knew that Reynolds was somewhere in America, but he was helpless as a child to find him. I offered to arrange his meeting with the gold-thief, if Guja would agree to give me some of the gold his tribe hoarded.

"He swore by the skull of the great leopard. I brought him secretly into these hills, and hid him up yonder in a shack the existence of which nobody suspects. It took me a wretched time to teach him just what he was to do--he'd no more brains than an ape. Night after night I went through the thing with him, until he learned the procedure: to watch in the hills until he saw a light flash in Reynolds' shack. Then steal down there, jerk the switch--and kill. These leopard men can see like cats at night.

"I called Reynolds up myself; it wasn't hard to imitate your voice. I used to do impersonations in vaudeville. While Guja was tearing the life out of Reynolds, I was dining at a well-known night club, in full sight of all.

"I came here tonight to smuggle him out of the country. But his blood-lust must have betrayed him. When he saw the light flash on in the cottage again, it must have started a train of associations that led him once more to the cottage, to kill whoever he found there. I saw the tag-end of the business--saw him stagger away from the shack, and then you follow him.

"Now then, I've shot the works. Nobody knows I'm mixed up in this business, but you. Will you keep your mouth shut and take a share of the Ekoi gold?"

The glow went out. In the sudden darkness, Brill, his pent-up feelings exploding at last, yelled: "Damn you, no! You murdering dog!" and sprang aside. The pistol cracked, an orange jet sliced the darkness, and the bullet fanned Brill's ear as he threw the heavy knife blindly. He heard it rattle futilely through the bushes, and stood frozen with the realization that he had lost his desperate gamble.

But even as he braced himself against the tearing impact of the bullet he expected, a sudden beam drilled the blackness, illuminating the convulsed features of John Galt.

"Don't move, Galt; I've got the drop on you."

It was the voice of Buckley. With a snarl, Galt took as desperate a chance as Brill had taken. He wheeled toward the source of the light, snapping down his automatic. But even as he did so, the detective's .45 crashed, and outlined against the brief glare, Galt swayed and fell like a tall tree struck by lightning.

"Dead?" asked the scientist, mechanically.

"Bullet tore through his forearm and smashed his shoulder," grunted Buckley. "Just knocked out temporarily. He'll live to decorate the gallows."

"You--you heard--?" Brill stuttered.

"Everything. I was just coming around the bend of the lake shore and saw a light in Reynolds' cottage, then your flash bobbing among the trees. I came sneaking through the bushes just in time to hear you give your translation of the nigger's dying words. I've been prowling around this lake all night."

"You suspected Galt all the time?"

The detective grinned wryly.

"I ought to say yes, and establish myself as a super sleuth. But the fact is, I suspected *you* all the time. That's why I came up here tonight--trying to figure out your connection with the murder. That alibi of yours was so iron-clad it looked phony to me. I had a sneaking suspicion that I'd bumped into a master-mind trying to put over the 'perfect crime.' I apologize! I've been reading too many detective stories lately!"

Moon of
Zambebwei

Chapter 1. The Horror in the Pines

The silence of the pine woods lay like a brooding cloak about the soul of Bristol McGrath. The black shadows seemed fixed, immovable as the weight of superstition that overhung this forgotten back-country. Vague ancestral dreads stirred at the back of McGrath's mind; for he was born in the pine woods, and sixteen years of roaming about the world had not erased their shadows. The fearsome tales at which he had shuddered as a child whispered again in his consciousness; tales of black shapes stalking the midnight glades . . . .

Cursing these childish memories, McGrath quickened his pace. The dim trail wound tortuously between dense walls of giant trees. No wonder he had been unable to hire anyone in the distant river village to drive him to the Ballville estate. The road was impassable for a vehicle, choked with rotting stumps and new growth. Ahead of him it bent sharply.

McGrath halted short, frozen to immobility. The silence had been broken at last, in such a way as to bring a chill tingling to the backs of his hands. For the sound had been the unmistakable groan of a human being in agony. Only for an instant was McGrath motionless. Then he was gliding about the bend of the trail with the noiseless slouch of a hunting panther.

A blue snub-nosed revolver had appeared as if by magic in his right hand. His left involuntarily clenched in his pocket on the bit of paper that was responsible for his presence in that grim forest. That paper was a frantic and mysterious appeal for aid; it was signed by McGrath's worst enemy, and contained the name of a woman long dead.

McGrath rounded the bend in the trail, every nerve tense and alert, expecting anything--except what he actually saw. His startled eyes hung on the grisly object for an instant, and then swept the forest walls. Nothing stirred there. A dozen feet back from the trail visibility vanished in a ghoulish twilight, where anything might lurk unseen. McGrath dropped to his knee beside the figure that lay in the trail before him.

It was a man, spread-eagled, hands and feet bound to four pegs driven deeply in the hard-packed earth; a blackbearded, hook-nosed, swarthy man. "Ahmed!", muttered McGrath. "Ballville's Arab Servant! God!"

For it was not the binding cords that brought the glaze to the Arab's eyes. A weaker man than McGrath might have sickened at the mutilations which keen knives had wrought on the man's body. McGrath recognized the work of an expert in the art of torture. Yet a spark of life still throbbed in the tough frame of the Arab. McGrath's gray eyes grew bleaker as he noted the position of the victim's body, and his mind flew back to another, grimmer jungle, and a half flayed black man pegged out on a path as a warning to the white man who dared invade a forbidden land.

He cut the cords, shifted the dying man to a more comfortable position. It was all he could do. He saw the delirium ebb momentarily in the bloodshot eyes, saw recognition glimmer there. Clots of bloody foam splashed the matted beard. The lips writhed soundlessly, and McGrath glimpsed the bloody stump of a severed tongue.

The black-nailed fingers began scrabbling in the dust. They shook, clawing erratically, but with purpose. McGrath bent close, tense with interest, and saw crooked lines grow under the quivering fingers. With the last effort of an iron will, the Arab was tracing a message in the characters of his own language. McGrath recognized the name: "Richard Ballville"; it was followed by "danger," and the hand waved weakly up the trail; then--and McGrath stiffened convulsively-- "Constance." One final effort of the dragging finger traced "John De Al--".

Suddenly the bloody frame was convulsed by one last sharp agony; the lean, sinewy hand knotted spasmodically and then fell limp. Ahmed ibn Suleyman was beyond vengeance or mercy.

McGrath rose, dusting his hands, aware of the tense stillness of the grim woods around him; aware of a faint rustling in their depths that was not caused by any breeze. He looked down at the mangled figure with involuntary pity, though he knew well the foulness of the Arab's heart, a black evil that had matched that of Ahmed's master, Richard Ballville. Well, it seemed that master and man had at last met their match in human fiendishness. But who, or what? For a hundred years the Ballvilles had ruled supreme over this back-country, first over their wide plantations and hundreds of slaves, and later over the submissive descendants of those slaves. Richard, the last of the Ballvilles, had exercised as much authority over the pinelands as any of his autocratic ancestors. Yet from this country where men had bowed to the Ballvilles for a century, had come that frenzied cry of fear, a telegram that McGrath clenched in his coat pocket.

Stillness succeeded the rustling, more sinister than any sound. McGrath knew he was watched; knew that the spot where Ahmed's body lay was the invisible deadline that had been drawn for him. He believed that he would be allowed to turn and retrace his steps unmolested to the distant village. He knew that if he continued on his way, death would strike him suddenly and unseen. Turning, he strode back the way he had come.

He made the turn and kept straight on until he had passed another crook in the trail. Then he halted, listened. All was silent. Quickly he drew the paper from his pocket, smoothed out the wrinkles and read, again, in the cramped scrawl of the man he hated most on earth:

Bristol:

If you still love Constance Brand, for God's sake forget your hate and come to Ballville Manor as quickly as the devil can drive you.

RICHARD BALLVILLE.

That was all. It reached him by telegraph in that Far Western city where McGrath had resided since his return from Africa. He would have ignored it, but for the mention of Constance Brand. That name had sent a choking, agonizing pulse of amazement through his soul, had sent him racing toward the land of his birth by train and plane, as if, indeed, the devil were on his heels. It was the name of one he thought dead for three years; the name of the only woman Bristol McGrath had ever loved.

Replacing the telegram, he left the trail and headed westward, pushing his powerful frame between the thickset trees. His feet made little sound on the matted pine needles. His progress was all but noiseless. Not for nothing had he spent his boyhood in the country of the big pines.

Three hundred yards from the old road he came upon that which he sought-an ancient trail paralleling the road. Choked with young growth, it was little more than a trace through the thick pines. He knew that it ran to the back of the Ballville mansion; did not believe the secret watchers would be guarding it. For how could they know he remembered it?

He hurried south along it, his ears whetted for any sound. Sight alone could not be trusted in that forest. The mansion, he knew, was not far away, now. He was passing through what had once been fields, in the days of Richard's grandfather, running almost up to the spacious lawns that girdled the Manor. But for half a century they had been abandoned to the advance of the forest.

But now he glimpsed the Manor, a hint of solid bulk among the pine tops ahead of him. And almost simultaneously his heart shot into his throat as a scream of human anguish knifed the stillness. He could not tell whether it was a man or a woman who screamed, and his thought that it might be a woman winged his feet in his reckless dash toward the building that loomed starkly up just beyond the straggling fringe of trees.

The young pines had even invaded the once generous lawns. The whole place wore an aspect of decay. Behind the Manor, the barns, and outhouses which once housed slave families, were crumbling in ruin. The mansion itself seemed to totter above the litter, a creaky giant, ratgnawed and rotting, ready to collapse at any untoward event. With the stealthy tread of a tiger Bristol McGrath approached a window on the side of the house. From that window sounds were issuing that were an affront to the tree-filtered sunlight and a crawling horror to the brain.

Nerving himself for what he might see, he peered within.

Chapter 2. Black Torture

He was looking into a great dusty chamber which might have served as a ballroom in ante-bellum days; its lofty ceiling was hung with cobwebs, its rich oak panels showed dark and stained. But there was a fire in the great fireplace-a small fire, just large enough to heat to a white glow the slender steel rods thrust into it.

But it was only later that Bristol McGrath saw the fire and the things that glowed on the hearth. His eyes were gripped like a spell on the master of the Manor; and once again he looked on a dying man.

A heavy beam had been nailed to the paneled wall, and from it jutted a rude cross-piece. From this cross-piece Richard Ballville hung by cords about his wrists. His toes barely touched the floor, tantalizingly, inviting him to stretch his frame continually in an effort to relieve the agonizing strain on his arms. The cords had cut deeply into his wrists; blood trickled down his arms; his hands were black and swollen almost to bursting. He was naked except for his trousers, and McGrath saw that already the white-hot irons had been horribly employed. There was reason enough for the deathly pallor of the man, the cold beads of agony upon his skin. Only his fierce vitality had allowed him thus long to survive the ghastly burns on his limbs and body.

On his breast had been burned a curious symbol-a cold hand laid itself on McGrath's spine. For he recognized that symbol, and once again his memory raced away across the world and the years to a black, grim, hideous jungle where drums bellowed in fire-shot darkness and naked priests of an abhorred cult traced a frightful symbol in quivering human flesh.

Between the fireplace and the dying man squatted a thick-set black man, clad only in ragged, muddy trousers.

His back was toward the window, presenting an impressive pair of shoulders. His bullet-head was set squarely between those gigantic shoulders, like that of a frog, and he appeared to be avidly watching the face of the man on the cross-piece.

Richard Ballville's bloodshot eyes were like those of a tortured animal, but they were fully sane and conscious: they blazed with desperate vitality. He lifted his head painfully and his gaze swept the room. Outside the window McGrath instinctively shrank back. He did not know whether Ballville saw him or not. The man showed no sign to betray the presence of the watcher to the bestial black who scrutinized him. Then the brute turned his head toward the fire, reaching a long ape-like arm toward a glowing iron-and Ballville's eyes blazed with a fierce and urgent meaning the watcher could not mistake. McGrath did not need the agonized motion of the tortured head that accompanied the look. With a tigerish bound he was over the window-sill and in the room, even as the startled black shot erect, whirling with apish agility.

McGrath had not drawn his gun. He dared not risk a shot that might bring other foes upon him. There was a butcher-knife in the belt that held up the ragged, muddy trousers. It seemed to leap like a living thing into the hand of the black as he turned. But in McGrath's hand gleamed a curved Afghan dagger that had served him well in many a bygone battle.

Knowing the advantage of instant and relentless attack, he did not pause. His feet scarcely touched the floor inside before they were hurling him at the astounded black man.

An inarticulate cry burst from the thick red lips. The eyes rolled wildly, the butcher-knife went back and hissed forward with the swiftness of a striking cobra that would have disembowled a man whose thews were less steely than those of Bristol McGrath.

But the black was involuntarily stumbling backward as he struck, and that instinctive action slowed his stroke just enough for McGrath to avoid it with a lightning-like twist of his torso. The long blade hissed under his arm-pit, slicing cloth and skin-and simultaneously the Afghan dagger ripped through the black, bull throat.

There was no cry, but only a choking gurgle as the man fell, spouting blood. McGrath had sprung free as a wolf springs after delivering the death-stroke. Without emotion he surveyed his handiwork. The black man was already dead, his head half severed from his body. That slicing sidewise lunge that slew in silence, severing the throat to the spinal column, was a favorite stroke of the hairy hillmen that haunt the crags overhanging the Khyber Pass. Less than a dozen white men have ever mastered it. Bristol McGrath was one.

McGrath turned to Richard Ballville. Foam dripped on the seared, naked breast, and blood trickled from the lips. McGrath feared that Ballville had suffered the same mutilation that had rendered Ahmed speechless; but it was only suffering and shock that numbed Ballville's tongue. McGrath cut his cords and eased him down on a worn old divan near by. Ballville's lean, muscle-corded body quivered like taut steel strings under McGrath's hands. He gagged, finding his voice.

"I knew you'd come!" he gasped, writhing at the contact of the divan against his seared flesh. "I've hated you for years, but I knew-"

McGrath's voice was harsh as the rasp of steel. "What did you mean by your mention of Constance Brand? She is dead."

A ghastly smile twisted the thin lips.

"No, she's not dead! But she soon will be, if you don't hurry. Quick! Brandy! There on the table-that beast didn't drink it all."

McGrath held the bottle to his lips; Ballville drank avidly. McGrath wondered at the man's iron nerve. That he was in ghastly agony was obvious. He should be screaming in a delirium of pain. Yet he held to sanity and spoke lucidly, though his voice was a laboring croak.

"I haven't much time," he choked. "Don't interrupt. Save your curses till later. We both loved Constance Brand. She loved you. Three years ago she disappeared. Her garments were found on the bank of a river. Her body was never recovered. You went to Africa to drown your sorrow; I retired to the estate of my ancestors and became a recluse.

"What you didn't know-what the world didn't know--was that Constance Brand came with me! No, she didn't drown. That ruse was my idea. For three years Constance Brand has lived in this house!" He achieved a ghastly laugh. "Oh, don't look so stunned, Bristol. She didn't come of her own free will. She loved you too much. I kidnapped her, brought her here by force-Bristol!" His voice rose to a frantic shriek. "If you kill me you'll never learn where she is!"

The frenzied hands that had locked on his corded throat relaxed and sanity returned to the red eyes of Bristol McGrath.

"Go on," he whispered in a voice not even he recognized.

"I couldn't help it," gasped the dying man. "She was the only woman I ever loved-oh, don't sneer, Bristol. The others didn't count. I brought her here where I was king. She couldn't escape, couldn't get word to the outside world. No one lives in this section except nigger

27

descendants of the slaves owned by my family. My word is-was-their only law.

"I swear I didn't harm her. I only kept her prisoner, trying to force her to marry me. I didn't want her any other way. I was mad, but I couldn't help it. I come of a race of autocrats who took what they wanted, recognized no law but their own desires. You know that. You understand it. You come of the same breed yourself.

"Constance hates me, if that's any consolation to you, damn you. She's strong, too. I thought I could break her spirit. But I couldn't, not without the whip, and I couldn't bear to use that." He grinned hideously at the wild growl that rose unbidden to McGrath's lips. The big man's eyes were coals of fire; his hard hands knotted into iron mallets.

A spasm racked Ballville, and blood started from his lips. His grin faded and he hurried on.

"All went well until the foul fiend inspired me to send for John De Albor. I met him in Vienna, years ago. He's from East Africa-a devil in human form! He saw Constance-lusted for her as only a man of his type can. When I finally realized that, I tried to kill him. Then I found that he was stronger than I; that he'd made himself master of the niggers-my niggers, to whom my word had always been law. He told them his devilish cult-'

"Voodoo," muttered McGrath involuntarily.

"No! Voodoo is infantile beside this black fiendishness. Look at the symbol on my breast, where De Albor burned it with a white-hot iron. You have been in Africa. You understand the brand of Zambebwei.

"De Albor turned my negroes against me. I tried to escape with Constance and Ahmed. My own blacks hemmed me in. I did smuggle a telegram through to the village by a man who remained faithful to me--they suspected him and tortured him until he admitted it. John De Albor brought me his head.

"Before the final break I hid Constance in a place where no one will ever find her, except you. De Albor tortured Ahmed until he told that I had sent for a friend of the girl's to aid us. Then De Albor sent his men up the road with what was left of Ahmed, as a warning to you if you came. It was this morning that they seized us; I hid Constance last night. Not even Ahmed knew where. De Albor tortured me to make me tell-" the dying man's hands clenched and a fierce passionate light blazed in his eyes. McGrath knew that not all the torments of all the hells could ever have wrung that secret from Ballville's iron lips.

"It was the least you could do," he said, his voice harsh with conflicting emotions. "I've lived in hell for three years because of you-and

Constance has. You deserve to die. If you weren't dying already I'd kill you myself."

"Damn you, do you think I want your forgiveness?" gasped the dying man. "I'm glad you suffered. If Constance didn't need your help, I'd like to see you dying as I'm dying-and I'll be waiting for you in hell. But enough of this. De Albor left me awhile to go up the road and assure himself that Ahmed was dead. This beast got to swilling my brandy and decided to torture me some himself.

"Now listen-Constance is hidden in Lost Cave. No man on earth knows of its existence except you and me not even the negroes. Long ago I put an iron door in the entrance, and I killed the man who did the work; so the secret is safe. There's no key. You've got to open it by working certain knobs."

It was more and more difficult for the man to enunciate intelligibly. Sweat dripped from his face, and the cords of his arms quivered.

"Run your fingers over the edge of the door until you find three knobs that form a triangle. You can't see them; you'll have to feel. Press each one in counter-clockwise motion, three times, around and around. Then pull on the bar. The door will open. Take Constance and fight your way out. If you see they're going to get you, shoot her! Don't let her fall into the hands of that black beast-"

The voice rose to a shriek, foam spattered from the livid writhing lips, and Richard Ballville heaved himself almost upright, then toppled limply back. The iron will that had animated the broken body had snapped at last, as a taut wire snaps.

McGrath looked down at the still form, his brain a maelstrom of seething emotions, then wheeled, glaring, every nerve atingle, his pistol springing into his hand.

Chapter 3. The Black Priest

A man stood in the doorway that opened upon the great outer hall-a tall man in a strange alien garb. He wore a turban and a silk coat belted with a gay-hued girdle. Turkish slippers were on his feet. His skin was not much darker than McGrath's, his features distinctly oriental in spite of the heavy glasses he wore.

"Who the devil are you?" demanded McGrath, covering him.

"Ali ibn Suleyman, effendi," answered the other in faultless Arabic. "I came to this place of devils at the urging of my brother, Ahmed ibn Suleyman, whose soul may the Prophet ease. In New Orleans the letter came to me. I hastened here. And lo, stealing through the woods, I saw black men dragging my brother's corpse to the river. I came on, seeking his master."

McGrath mutely indicated the dead man. The Arab bowed his head in stately reverence.

"My brother loved him," he said. "I would have vengeance for my brother and my brother's master. Ef fendi, let me go with you."

"All right." McGrath was afire with impatience. He knew the fanatical clan-loyalty of the Arabs, knew that Ahmed's one decent trait had been a fierce devotion for the scoundrel he served. "Follow me."

With a last glance at the master of the Manor and the black body sprawling like a human sacrifice before him, McGrath left the chamber of torture. Just so, he reflected,' one of Ballville's warrior-king ancestors might have lain in some dim past age, with a slaughtered slave at his feet to serve his spirit in the land of ghosts.

With the Arab at his heels, McGrath emerged into the girdling pines that slumbered in the still heat of the noon. Faintly to his ears a distant pulse of sound was borne by a vagrant drift of breeze. It sounded like the throb of a faraway drum.

"Come on!" McGrath strode through the cluster of outhouses and plunged into the woods that rose behind them. Here, too, had once stretched the fields that builded the wealth of the aristocratic Ballvilles; but for many years they had been abandoned. Paths straggled aimlessly through the ragged growth, until presently the growing denseness of the trees told the invaders that they were in forest that had never known the woodsman's ax. McGrath looked for a path. Impressions received in childhood are always enduring. Memory remains, overlaid by later things, but unerring through the years. McGrath found the path he sought, a dim trace, twisting through the trees.

They were forced to walk single file; the branches scraped their clothing, their feet sank into the carpet of pine needles. The land trended gradually lower. Pines gave way to cypresses, choked with underbrush. Scummy pools of stagnant water glimmered under the trees. Bullfrogs croaked, mosquitoes sang with maddening insistence about them. Again the distant drum throbbed across the pinelands.

McGrath shook the sweat out of his eyes. That drum roused memories well fitted to these somber surroundings. His thoughts reverted to the hideous scar seared on Richard Ballville's naked breast. Ballville had supposed that he, McGrath, knew its meaning; but he did not. That it portended black horror and madness he knew, but its full significance he did not know. Only once before had he seen that symbol, in the horror-haunted country of Zambebwei, into which few white men had ever ventured, and from which only one white man had ever escaped alive. Bristol McGrath was that man, and he had only penetrated the fringe of that abysmal land of jungle and black swamp. He had not been able to plunge deep enough into that forbidden realm either to prove or to disprove the ghastly tales men whispered of an ancient cult surviving a prehistoric age, of the worship of a monstrosity whose mold violated an accepted law of nature. Little enough he had seen; but what he had seen had filled him with shuddering horror that sometimes returned now in crimson nightmares.

No word had passed between the men since they had left the Manor. McGrath plunged on through the vegetation that choked the path. A fat, blunt-tailed moccasin slithered from under his feet and vanished. Water could not be far away; a few more steps revealed it. They stood on the edge of a dank, slimy marsh from which rose a miasma of rotting vegetable matter. Cypresses shadowed it. The path ended at its edge. The swamp stretched away and away, lost to sight swiftly in twilight dimness.

"What now, effendi?" asked Ali. "Are we to swim this morass?"

"It's full of bottomless quagmires," answered McGrath. "It would be suicide for a man to plunge into it. Not even the piny woods niggers have ever tried to cross it. But there is a way to get to the hill that rises in the middle of it. You can just barely glimpse it, among the branches of the cypresses, see? Years ago, when Ballville and I were boys-and friends--we discovered an old, old Indian path, a secret, submerged road that led to that hill. There's a cave in the hill, and a woman is imprisoned in that cave. I'm going to it. Do you want to follow me, or to wait for me here? The path is a dangerous one."

"I will go, effendi," answered the Arab.

McGrath nodded in appreciation, and began to scan the trees about him. Presently he found what he was looking for a faint blaze on a huge cypress, an old mark, almost imperceptible. Confidently then, he stepped into the marsh beside the tree. He himself had made that mark, long ago. Scummy water rose over his shoe soles, but no higher. He stood on a flat rock, or rather on a heap of rocks, the topmost of which was just below the stagnant surface. Locating a certain gnarled cypress far out in the shadow of the marsh, he began walking directly toward it, spacing his strides carefully, each carrying him to a rockstep invisible below the murky water. Ali ibn Suleyman followed him, imitating his motions.

Through the swamp they went, following the marked trees that were their guide-posts. McGrath wondered anew at the motives that had impelled the ancient builders of the trail to bring these huge rocks from afar and sink them like piles into the slush. The work must have been stupendous, requiring no mean engineering skill. Why had the Indians built this broken road to Lost Island? Surely that isle and the cave in it had some religious significance to the red men; or perhaps it was their refuge against some stronger foe.

The going was slow; a misstep meant a plunge into marshy ooze, into unstable mire that might swallow a man alive. The island grew out of the trees ahead of them-a small knoll, girdled by a vegetation-choked beach. Through the foliage was visible the rocky wall that rose sheer from the beach to a height of fifty or sixty feet. It was almost like a granite block rising from a flat sandy rim. The pinnacle was almost bare of growth.

McGrath was pale, his breath coming in quick gasps. As they stepped upon the beach-like strip, Ali, with a glance of commiseration, drew a flask from his pocket.

"Drink a little brandy, effendi," he urged, touching the mouth to his own lips, oriental-fashion. "It will aid you."

McGrath knew that Ali thought his evident agitation was a result of exhaustion. But he was scarcely aware of his recent exertions. It was the emotions that raged within him-the thought of Constance Brand, whose beautiful form had haunted his troubled dreams for three dreary years. He gulped deeply of the liquor, scarcely tasting it, and handed back the flask.

"Come on!"

The pounding of his own heart was suffocating, drowning the distant drum, as he thrust through the choking vegetation at the foot of the cliff. On the gray rock above the green mask appeared a curious carven symbol, as he had seen it years ago, when its discovery led him and Richard Ballville to the hidden cavern. He tore aside the clinging vines and fronds, and his breath sucked in at the sight of a heavy iron door set in the narrow mouth that opened in the granite wall.

McGrath's fingers were trembling as they swept over the metal, and behind him he could hear Ali breathing heavily. Some of the white man's excitement had imparted itself to the Arab. McGrath's hands found the three knobs, forming the apices of a triangle-mere protuberances, not apparent to the sight. Controlling his jumping nerves, he pressed them as Ballville had instructed him, and felt each give slightly at the third pressure. Then, holding his breath, he grasped the bar that was welded in the middle of the door, and pulled. Smoothly, on oiled hinges, the massive portal swung open.

They looked into a wide tunnel that ended in another door, this a grille of steel bars. The tunnel was not dark; it was clean and roomy, and the ceiling had been pierced to allow light to enter, the holes covered with screens to keep out insects and reptiles. But through the grille he glimpsed something that sent him racing along the tunnel, his heart almost bursting through his ribs. Ali was close at his heels.

The grille-door was not locked. It swung outward under his fingers. He stood motionless, almost stunned with the impact of his emotions.

His eyes were dazzled by a gleam of gold; a sunbeam slanted down through the pierced rock roof and struck mellow fire from the glorious profusion of golden hair that flowed over the white arm that pillowed the beautiful head on the carved oak table.

"Constance!" It was a cry of hunger and yearning that burst from his livid lips.

Echoing the cry, the girl started up, staring wildly, her hands at her temples, her lambent hair rippling over her shoulders. To his dizzy gaze she seemed to float in an aureole of golden light.

"Bristol! Bristol McGrath!" she echoed his call with a haunting, incredulous cry. Then she was in his arms, her white arms clutching him in a frantic embrace, as if she feared he were but a phantom that might vanish from her.

For the moment the world ceased to exist for Bristol McGrath. He might have been blind, deaf and dumb to the universe at large. His dazed brain was cognizant only of the woman in his arms, his senses drunken' with the softness and fragrance of her, his soul stunned with the overwhelming realization of a dream he had thought dead and vanished for ever.

When he could think consecutively again, he shook himself like a man coming out of a trance, and stared stupidly around him. He was in a wide chamber, cut in the solid rock. Like the tunnel, it was illumined from above, and the air was fresh and clean. There were chairs, tables and a hammock, carpets on the rocky floor, cans of food and a water-cooler. Ballville had not failed to provide for his captive's comfort. McGrath glanced around at the Arab, and saw him beyond the grille. Considerately he had not intruded upon their reunion.

"Three years!" the girl was sobbing. "Three years I've waited. I knew you'd come! I knew it! But we must be careful, my darling. Richard will kill you if he finds you kill us both!"

"He's beyond killing anyone," answered McGrath. "But just the same, we've got to get out of here."

Her eyes flared with new terror.

"Yes! John De Albor! Ballville was afraid of him. That's why he locked me in here. He said he'd sent for you. I was afraid for you-"

"Ali!" McGrath called. "Come in here. We're getting out of here now, and we'd better take some water and food with us. We may have to hide in the swamps for-"

Abruptly Constance shrieked, tore herself from her lover's arms. And McGrath, frozen by the sudden, awful fear in her wide eyes, felt the dull jolting impact of a savage blow at the base of his skull. Consciousness did not leave him, but a strange paralysis gripped him. He dropped like an empty sack on the stone floor and lay there like a dead man, helplessly staring up at the scene which tinged his brain with madness-Constance struggling frenziedly in the grasp of the man he had known as Ali ibn Suleyman, now terribly transformed.

34

The man had thrown off his turban and glasses. And in the murky whites of his eyes, McGrath read the truth with its grisly implications-the man was not an Arab. He was a negroid mixed breed. Yet some of his blood must have been Arab, for there was a slightly Semitic cast to his countenance, and this cast, together with his oriental garb and his perfect acting of his part, had made him seem genuine. But now all this was discarded and the negroid strain was uppermost; even his voice, which had enunciated the sonorous Arabic, was now the throaty gutturals of the negro.

"You've killed him!" the girl sobbed hysterically, striving vainly to break away from the cruel fingers that prisoned her white wrists.

"He's not dead yet," laughed the octoroon. "The fool quaffed drugged brandy-a drug found only in the Zambebwei jungles. It lies inactive in the system until made effective by a sharp blow on a nerve center."

"Please do something for him!" she begged.

The fellow laughed brutally.

"Why should I? He has served his purpose. Let him lie there until the swamp insects have picked his bones. I should like to watch that-but we will be far away before nightfall." His eyes blazed with the bestial gratification of possession. The sight of this white beauty struggling in his grasp seemed to rouse all the jungle lust in the man. McGrath's wrath and agony found expression only in his bloodshot eyes. He could not move hand or foot.

"It was well I returned alone to the Manor," laughed the octoroon. "I stole up to the window while this fool talked with Richard Ballville. The thought came to me to let him lead me to the place where you were hidden. It had never occurred to me that there was a hiding-place in the swamp. I had the Arab's coat, slippers and turban; I had thought I might use them sometime. The glasses helped, too. It was not difficult to make an Arab out of myself. This man had never seen John De Albor. I was born in East Africa and grew up a slave in the house of an Arab before I ran away and wandered to the land of Zambebwei.

"But enough. We must go. The drum has been muttering all day. The blacks are restless. I promised them a sacrifice to Zemba. I was going to use the Arab, but by the time I had tortured out of him the information I desired, he was no longer fit for a sacrifice. Well, let them bang their silly drum. They'd like to have you for the Bride of Zemba, but they don't know I've found you. I have a motor-boat hidden on the river five miles from here-"

"You fool!" shrieked Constance, struggling passionately. "Do you think you can carry a white girl down the river, like a slave?"

"I have a drug which will make you like a dead woman," he said. "You will lie in the bottom of the boat, covered by sacks. When I board the steamer that shall bear us from these shores, you will go into my cabin in a large, well-ventilated trunk. You will know nothing of the discomforts of the voyage. You will awake in Africa--"

He was fumbling in his shirt, necessarily releasing her with one hand. With a frenzied scream and a desperate wrench, she tore loose and sped out through the tunnel. John De Albor plunged after her, bellowing. A red haze floated before McGrath's maddened eyes. The girl would plunge to her death in the swamps, unless she remembered the guide-marks--perhaps it was death she sought, in preference to the fate planned for her by the fiendish negro.

They had vanished from his sight, out of the tunnel; but suddenly Constance screamed again, with a new poignancy. To McGrath's ears came an excited jabbering of negro gutturals. De Albor's accents were lifted in angry protest. Constance was sobbing hysterically. The voices were moving away. McGrath got a vague glimpse of a group of figures through the masking vegetation as they moved across the line of the tunnel mouth. He saw Constance being dragged along by half a dozen giant blacks typical pineland dwellers, and after them came John De Albor, his hands eloquent in dissension. That glimpse only, through the fronds, and then the tunnel mouth gaped empty and the sound of splashing water faded away through 'the marsh.

Chapter 4. The Black God's Hunger

In the brooding silence of the cavern Bristol McGrath lay staring blankly upward, his soul a seething hell. Fool, fool, to be taken in so easily! Yet, how could he have known? He had never seen De Albor; he had supposed he was a full-blooded negro. Ballville had called him a black beast, but he must have been referring to his soul. De Albor, but for the betraying murk of his eyes, might pass anywhere for a white man.

The presence of those black men meant but one thing: they had followed him and De Albor, had seized Constance as she rushed from the cave. De Albor's evident fear bore a hideous implication; he had said the blacks wanted to sacrifice Constance-now she was in their hands.

"God!" The word burst from McGrath's lips, startling in the stillness, startling to the speaker. He was electrified; a few moments before he had been dumb. But now he discovered he could move his lips, his tongue. Life was stealing back through his dead limbs; they stung as if with returning circulation. Frantically he encouraged that sluggish flow. Laboriously he worked his extremities, his fingers, hands, wrists and finally, with a surge of wild triumph, his arms and legs. Perhaps De Albor's hellish drug had lost some of its power through age. Perhaps McGrath's unusual stamina threw off the effects as another man could not have done.

The tunnel door had not been closed, and McGrath knew why; they did not want to shut out the insects which would soon dispose of a helpless body; already the pests were streaming through the door, a noisome horde.

McGrath rose at last, staggering drunkenly, but with his vitality surging more strongly each second. When he tottered from the cave, no living thing met his glare. Hours had passed since the negroes had departed with their prey. He strained his ears for the drum. It was silent. The stillness rose like an invisible black mist around him. Stumblingly he splashed along the rock-trail that led to hard ground. Had the blacks taken their captive back to the death-haunted Manor, or deeper into the pinelands?

Their tracks were thick in the mud: half a dozen pairs of bare, splay feet, the slender prints of Constance's shoes, the marks of De Albor's Turkish slippers. He followed them with increasing difficulty as the ground grew higher and harder.

He would have missed the spot where they turned off the dim trail but for the fluttering of a bit of silk in the faint breeze. Constance had brushed against a tree-trunk there, and the rough bark had shredded off a fragment of her dress. The band had been headed east, toward the Manor. At the spot where the bit of cloth hung, they had turned sharply southward. The matted pine needles showed no tracks, but disarranged vines and branches bent aside marked their progress, until McGrath, following these signs, came out upon another trail leading southward.

Here and there were marshy spots, and these showed the prints of feet, bare and shod. McGrath hastened along the trail, pistol in hand, in full possession of his faculties at last. His face was grim and pale. De Albor had not had an opportunity to disarm him after striking that treacherous blow. Both the octoroon and the blacks of the pinelands believed him to be lying helpless back in Lost Cave. That, at least, was to his advantage.

He kept straining his ears in vain for the drum he had heard earlier in the day. The silence did not reassure him. In a voodoo sacrifice drums would be thundering, but he knew he was dealing with something even more ancient and abhorrent than voodoo.

Voodoo was comparatively a young religion, after all, born in the hills of Haiti. Behind the froth of voodooism rose the grim religions of Africa, like granite cliffs glimpsed through a mask of green fronds. Voodooism was a mewling infant beside the black, immemorial colossus that had reared its terrible shape in the older land through uncounted ages, Zambebwei! The very name sent a shudder through him, symbolic of horror and fear. It was more than the name of a country and the mysterious tribe that inhabited that country; it signified something fearfully old and evil, something that had survived its natural epoch-a religion of the Night, and a deity whose name was Death and Horror.

38

He had seen no negro cabins. He knew these were farther to the east and south, most of them, huddling along the banks of the river and the tributary creeks. It was the instinct of the black man to build his habitation by a river, as he had built by the Congo, the Nile and the Niger since Time's first gray dawn. Zambebwei! The word beat like a throb of a tom-tom through the brain of Bristol McGrath. The soul of the black man had not changed, through the slumberous centuries. Change might come in the clangor of city streets, in the raw rhythms of Harlem; but the swamps of the Mississippi do not differ enough from the swamps of the Congo to work any great transmutation in the spirit of a race that was old before the first white king wove the thatch of his wattled hut-palace.

Following that winding path through the twilight dimness of the big pines, McGrath did not find it in his soul to marvel that black slimy tentacles from the depths of Africa had stretched across the world to breed nightmares in an alien land. Certain natural conditions produce certain effects, breed certain pestilences of body or mind, regardless of their geographical situation. The river-haunted pinelands were as abysmal in their way as were the reeking African jungles.

The trend of the trail was away from the river. The land sloped very gradually upward, and all signs of marsh vanished.

The trail widened, showing signs of frequent use. McGrath became nervous. At any moment he might meet someone. He took to the thick woods alongside the trail, and forced his way onward, each movement sounding cannon-loud to his whetted ears. Sweating with nervous tension, he came presently upon a smaller path, which meandered in the general direction he wished to go. The pinelands were crisscrossed by such paths.

He followed it with greater ease and stealth, and presently, coming to a crook in it, saw it join the main trail. Near the point of junction stood a small log cabin, and between him and the cabin squatted a big black man. This man was hidden behind the bole of a huge pine beside the narrow path, and peering around it toward the cabin. Obviously he was spying on someone, and it was quickly apparent who this was, as John De Albor came to the door and stared despairingly down the wide trail. The black watcher stiffened and lifted his fingers to his mouth as if to sound a far-carrying whistle, but De Albor shrugged his shoulders helplessly and turned back into the cabin again. The negro relaxed, though he did not alter his vigilance.

What this portended, McGrath did not know, nor did he pause to speculate. At the sight of De Albor a red mist turned the sunlight to blood, in which the black body before him floated like an ebony goblin.

A panther stealing upon its kill would have made as much noise as McGrath made in his glide down the path toward the squatting black. He was aware of no personal animosity toward the man, who was but an obstacle in his path of vengeance. Intent on the cabin, the black man did not hear that stealthy approach. Oblivious to all else, he did not move or turn-until the pistol butt descended on his woolly skull with an impact that stretched him senseless among the pine needles.

McGrath crouched above his motionless victim, listening. There was no sound near by-but suddenly, far away, there rose a long-drawn shriek that shuddered and died away. The blood congealed in McGrath's veins. Once before he had heard that sound-in the low forest-covered hills that fringe the borders of forbidden Zambebwei; his black boys had turned the color of ashes and fallen on their faces. What it was he did not know; and the explanation offered by the shuddering natives had been too monstrous to be accepted by a rational mind. They called it the voice of the god of Zambebwei.

Stung to action, McGrath rushed down the path and hurled himself against the back door of the cabin. He did not know how many blacks were inside; he did not care. He was berserk with grief and fury.

The door crashed inward under the impact. He lit on his feet inside, crouching, gun leveled hip-high, lips asnarl.

But only one man faced him--John De Albor, who sprang to his feet with a startled cry. The gun dropped from McGrath's fingers. Neither lead nor steel could glut his hate now. It must be with naked hands, turning back the pages of civilization to the red dawn days of the primordial.

With a growl that was less like the cry of a man than the grunt of a charging lion, McGrath's fierce hands locked about the octoroon's throat. De Albor was borne backward by the hurtling impact, and the men crashed together over a camp cot, smashing it to ruins. And as they tumbled on the dirt floor, McGrath set himself to kill his enemy with his bare fingers.

The octoroon was a tall man, rangy and strong. But against the berserk white man he had no chance. He was hurled about like a sack of straw, battered and smashed savagely against the floor, and the iron fingers that were crushing his throat sank deeper and deeper until his tongue protruded from his gaping blue lips and his eyes were starting from his head. With death no more than a hand's breadth from the octoroon, some measure of sanity returned to McGrath.

He shook his head like a dazed bull; eased his terrible grip a trifle, and snarled: "Where is the girl? Quick, before I kill you!"

De Albor retched and fought for breath, ashen-faced. "The blacks!" he gasped. "They have taken her to be the Bride of Zemba! I could not prevent them. They demand a sacrifice. I offered them you, but they said you were paralyzed and would die anyway-they were cleverer than I thought. They followed me back to the Manor from the spot where we left, the Arab in the road-followed us from the Manor to the island.

"They are out of hand-mad with blood-lust. But even I, who know black men as none else knows them, I had forgotten that not even a priest of Zambebwei can control them when the fire of worship runs in their veins. I am their priest and master-yet when I sought to save the girl, they forced me into this cabin and set a man to watch me until the sacrifice is over. You must have killed him; he would never have let you enter here."

With a chill grimness, McGrath picked up his pistol.

"You came here as Richard Ballville's friend," he said unemotionally. "To get possession of Constance Brand, you made devil-worshippers out of the black people. You deserve death for that. When the European authorities that govern Africa catch a priest of Zambebwei, they hang him. You have admitted that you are a priest. Your life is forfeit on that score, too. But it is because of your hellish teachings that Constance Brand is to die, and it's for that reason that I'm going to blow out your brains."

John De Albor shriveled. "She is not dead yet," he gasped, great drops of perspiration dripping from his ashy face. "She will not die until the moon is high above the pines. It is full tonight, the Moon of Zambebwei. Don't kill me. Only I can save her. I know I failed before. But if I go to them, appear to them suddenly and without warning, they'll think it is because of supernatural powers that I was able to escape from the but without being seen by the watchman. That will renew my prestige.

"You can't save her. You might shoot a few blacks, but there would still be scores left to kill you-and her. But I have a plan-yes, I am a priest of Zambebwei. When I was a boy I ran away from my Arab master and wandered far until I came to the land of Zambebwei. There I grew to manhood and became a priest, dwelling there until the white blood in me drew me out in the world again to learn the ways of the white men. When I came to America I brought a Zemba with me-I can not tell you how.

"Let me save Constance Brand!" He was clawing at McGrath, shaking as if with an ague. "I love her, even as you love her. I will play fair with you both, I swear it! Let me save her! We can fight for her later, and I'll kill you if I can."

The frankness of that statement swayed McGrath more than anything else the octoroon could have said. It was a desperate gamble-but after all, Constance would be no worse off with John De Albor alive than she was already. She would be dead before midnight unless something was done swiftly.

"Where is the place of sacrifice?" asked McGrath.

"Three miles away, in an open glade," answered De Albor. "South on the trail that runs past my cabin. All the blacks are gathered there except my guard and some others who are watching the trail below the cabin. They are scattered out along it, the nearest out of sight of my cabin, but within sound of the loud, shrill whistle with which these people signal one another.

"This is my plan. You wait here in my cabin, or in the woods, as you choose. I'll avoid the watchers on the trail, and appear suddenly before the blacks at the House of Zemba. A sudden appearance will impress them deeply, as I said. I know I can not persuade them to abandon their plan, but I will make them postpone the sacrifice until just before dawn. And before that time I will manage to steal the girl and flee with her. I'll return to your hiding-place, and we'll fight our way out together."

McGrath laughed. "Do you think I'm an utter fool? You'd send your blacks to murder me, while you carried Constance away as you planned. I'm going with you. I'll hide at the edge of the clearing, to help you if you need help. And if you make a false move, I'll get you, if I don't get anybody else."

The octoroon's murky eyes glittered, but he nodded acquiescence.

"Help me bring your guard into the cabin," said McGrath. "He'll be coming to soon. We'll tie and gag him and leave him here."

The sun was setting and twilight was stealing over the pinelands as McGrath and his strange companion stole through the shadowy woods. They had circled to the west to avoid the watchers on the trail, and were now following on the many narrow footpaths which traced their way through the forest. Silence reigned ahead of them, and McGrath mentioned this.

"Zemba is a god of silence," muttered De Albor. "From sunset to sunrise on the night of the full moon, no drum is beaten. If a dog barks, it must be slain; if a baby cries, it must be killed. Silence locks

42

the jaws of the people until Zemba roars. Only his voice is lifted on the night of the Moon of Zemba."

McGrath shuddered. The foul deity was an intangible spirit, of course, embodied only in legend; but De Albor spoke of it as a living thing.

A few stars were blinking out, and shadows crept through the thick woods, blurring the trunks of the trees that melted together in darkness. McGrath knew they could not be far from the House of Zemba. He sensed the close presence of a throng of people, though he heard nothing.

De Albor, ahead of him, halted suddenly, crouching. McGrath stopped, trying to pierce the surrounding mask of interlacing branches.

"What is it?" muttered the white man, reaching for his pistol.

De Albor shook his head, straightening. McGrath could not see the stone in his hand, caught up from the earth as he stooped.

"Do you hear something?" demanded McGrath.

De Albor motioned him to lean forward, as if to whisper in his ear. Caught off his guard, McGrath bent toward him-even so he divined the treacherous African's intention, but it was too late. The stone in De Albor's hand crashed sickeningly against the white man's temple. McGrath went down like a slaughtered ox, and De Albor sped away down the path to vanish like a ghost in the gloom.

Chapter 5. The Voice of Zemba

In the darkness of the woodland path McGrath stirred at last, and staggered groggily to his feet. That desperate blow might have crushed the skull of a man whose physique and vitality were not that of a bull. His head throbbed and there was dried blood on his temple; but his strongest sensation was burning scorn at himself for having again fallen victim to John De Albor. And yet, who would have suspected that move? He knew De Albor would kill him if he could, but he had not expected an attack before the rescue of Constance. The fellow was dangerous and unpredictable as a cobra. Had his pleas to be allowed to attempt Constance's rescue been but a ruse to escape death at the hands of McGrath?

McGrath stared dizzily at the stars that gleamed through the ebon branches, and sighed with relief to see that the moon had not yet risen. The pinewoods were black as only pinelands can be, with a darkness that was almost tangible, like a substance that could be cut with a knife.

McGrath had reason to be grateful for his rugged constitution. Twice that day had John De Albor outwitted him, and twice the white man's iron frame had survived the attack. His gun was in his scabbard, his knife in its sheath. De Albor had not paused to search, had not paused for a second stroke to make sure. Perhaps there had been a tinge of panic in the African's actions.

Well,--this did not change matters a great deal. He believed that De Albor would make an effort to save the girl. And McGrath intended to be on hand, whether to play a lone hand, or to aid the octoroon. This was no time to hold grudges, with the girl's life at stake. He groped down the path, spurred by a rising glow in the east.

He came upon the glade almost before he knew it. The moon hung in the low branches, blood-red, high enough to illumine it and the throng of black people who squatted in a vast semicircle about it, facing the moon. Their rolling eyes gleamed milkily in the shadows, their features were grotesque masks. None spoke. No head turned toward the bushes behind which he crouched.

He had vaguely expected blazing fires, a blood-stained altar, drums and the chant of maddened worshippers; that would be voodoo. But this was not voodoo, and there was a vast gulf between the two cults. There were no fires, no altars. But the breath hissed through his locked teeth. In a far land he had sought in vain for the rituals of Zambebwei; now he looked upon them within forty miles of the spot where he was born.

In the center of the glade the ground rose slightly to a flat level. On this stood a heavy iron-bound stake that was indeed but the sharpened trunk of a good-sized pine driven deep into the ground. And there was something living chained to that stake-something which caused McGrath to catch his breath in horrified unbelief.

He was looking upon a god of Zambebwei. Stories had told of such creatures, wild tales drifting down from the borders of the forbidden country, repeated by shivering natives about jungle fires, passed along until they reached the ears of skeptical white traders. McGrath had never really believed the stories, though he had gone searching for the being they described. For they spoke of a beast that was a blasphemy against nature-a beast that sought food strange to its natural species.

The thing chained to the stake was an ape, but such an ape as the world at large never dreamed of, even in nightmares. Its shaggy gray hair was shot with silver that shone in the rising moon; it looked gigantic as it squatted ghoulishly on its haunches. Upright, on its bent, gnarled legs, it would be as tall as a man, and much broader and thicker. But its prehensile fingers were armed with talons like those of a tiger-not the heavy blunt nails of the natural anthropoid, but the cruel scimitar-curved claws of the great carnivora. Its face was like that of a gorilla, low browed, flaring-nostriled, chinless; but when it snarled, its wide flat nose wrinkled like that of a great cat, and the cavernous mouth disclosed saber-like fangs, the fangs of a beast of prey. This was Zemba, the creature sacred to the people of the land of Zambebwei-a monstrosity, a violation of an accepted law of nature-a carnivorous ape. Men had laughed at the story, hunters and zoologists and traders.

But now McGrath knew that such creatures dwelt in black Zambebwei and were worshipped, as primitive man is prone to worship an obscenity or perversion of nature. Or a survival of past eons: that was what the flesh-eating apes of Zambebwei were-survivors of a forgotten epoch, remnants of a vanished prehistoric age, when nature was experimenting with matter, and life took many monstrous forms.

The sight of the monstrosity filled McGrath with revulsion; it was abysmal, a reminder of that brutish and horror shadowed past out of which mankind crawled so painfully, eons ago. This thing was an affront to sanity; it belonged in the dust of oblivion with the dinosaur, the mastodon, and the saber-toothed tiger.

It looked massive beyond the stature of modern beasts-shaped on the plan of another age, when all things were cast in a mightier mold. He wondered if the revolver at his hip would have any effect on it; wondered by what dark and subtle means John De Albor had brought the monster from Zambebwei to the pinelands.

But something was happening in the glade, heralded by the shaking of the brute's chain as it thrust forward its nightmare=head.

From the shadows of the trees came a file of black men and women, young, naked except for a mantle of monkey skins and parrot-feathers thrown over the shoulders of each. More regalia brought by John De Albor, undoubtedly. They formed a semicircle at a safe distance from the chained brute, and sank to their knees, bending their heads to the ground before him. Thrice this motion was repeated. Then, rising, they formed two lines, men and women facing one another, and began to dance; at least it might by courtesy be called a dance. They hardly moved their feet at all, but all other parts of their bodies were in constant motion, twisting, rotating, writhing. The measured, rhythmical movements had no connection at all with the voodoo dances McGrath had witnessed. This dance was disquietingly archaic in its suggestion, though even more depraved and bestial-naked primitive passions framed in a cynical debauchery of motion.

No sound came from the dancers, or from the votaries squatting about the ring of trees. But the ape, apparently infuriated by the continued movements, lifted his head and sent into the night the frightful shriek McGrath had heard once before that day-he had heard it in the hills that border black Zambebwei. The brute plunged to the end of his heavy chain, foaming and gnashing his fangs, and the dancers fled like spume blown before a gust of wind. They scattered in all directions-- and then McGrath started up in his covert, barely stifling a cry.

From the deep shadows had come a figure, gleaming tawnily in contrast to the black forms about it. It was John De Albor, naked except for a mantle of bright feathers, and on his head a circlet of gold that might have been forged in Atlantis. In his hand he bore a gold wand that was the scepter of the high priests of Zambebwei.

Behind him came a pitiful figure, at the sight of which the moon-lit forest reeled to McGrath's sight.

Constance had been drugged. Her face was that of a sleep-walker; she seemed not aware of her peril, or the fact that she was naked. She walked like a robot, mechanically responding to the urge of the cord tied about her white neck. The other end of that cord was in John De Albor's hand, and he half led, half dragged her toward the horror that squatted in the center of the glade. De Albor's face was ashy in the moonlight that now flooded the glade with molten silver. Sweat beaded his skin. His eyes gleamed with fear and ruthless determination. And in a staggering instant McGrath knew that the man had failed, that he had been unable to save Constance, and that now, to save his own life from his suspicious followers, he himself was dragging the girl to the gory sacrifice.

No vocal sound came from the votaries, but hissing intake of breath sucked through thick lips, and the rows of black bodies swayed like reeds in the wind. The great ape leaped up, his face a slavering devil's mask; he howled with frightful eagerness, gnashing his great fangs, that yearned to sink into that soft white flesh, and the hot blood beneath. He surged against his chain, and the stout post quivered. McGrath, in the bushes, stood frozen, paralyzed by the imminence of horror. And then John De Albor stepped behind the unresisting girl and gave her a powerful push that sent her reeling forward to pitch headlong on the ground under the monster's talons.

And simultaneously McGrath moved. His move was instinctive rather than conscious. His .44 jumped into his hand and spoke, and the great ape screamed like a man death-stricken and reeled, clapping misshapen hands to its head.

An instant the throng crouched frozen, white eyes bulging, jaws hanging slack. Then before any could move, the ape, blood gushing from his head, wheeled, seized the chain in both hands and snapped it with a wrench that twisted the heavy links apart as if they had been paper.

John De Albor stood directly before the mad brute, paralyzed in his tracks. Zemba roared and leaped, and the African went down under him, disembowled by the razorlike talons, his head crushed to a crimson pulp by a sweep of the great paw.

Ravening, the monster charged among the votaries, clawing and ripping and smiting, screaming intolerably. Zambebwei spoke, and death was in his bellowing Screaming, howling, fighting, the black people scrambled over one another in their mad flight. Men and women went down under those shearing talons, were dismembered by those gnashing fangs. It was a red drama of the primitive-destruction amuck and ariot, the primordial embodied in fangs and talons, gone mad and plunging in slaughter. Blood and brains deluged the earth, black bodies and limbs and fragments of bodies littered the moonlighted glade in ghastly heaps before the last of the howling wretches found refuge among the trees. The sounds of their blundering, panic-stricken flight drifted back.

McGrath had leaped from his covert almost as soon as he had fired. Unnoticed by the terrified negroes, and himself scarcely cognizant of the slaughter raging around him, he raced across the glade toward the pitiful white figure that lay limply beside the iron-bound stake.

"Constance!" he cried, gathering her to his breast.

Languidly she opened her cloudy eyes. He held her close, heedless of the screams and devastation surging about them. Slowly recognition grew in those lovely eyes.

"Bristol!" she murmured, incoherently. Then she screamed, clung to him, sobbing hysterically. "Bristol! They told me you were dead! The blacks! The horrible blacks! They're going to kill me! They were going to kill De Albor too, but he promised to sacrifice-"

"Don't, girl, don't!" He subdued her frantic tremblings. "It's all right, now-" Abruptly he looked up into the grinning bloodstained face of nightmare and death. The great ape had ceased to rend his dead victims and was slinking toward the living pair in the center of the glade. Blood oozed from the wound in its sloping skull that had maddened it.

McGrath sprang toward it, shielding the prostrate girl; his pistol spurted flame, pouring a stream of lead into the mighty breast as the beast charged.

On it came, and his confidence waned. Bullet after bullet he sent crashing into its vitals, but it did not halt. Now he dashed the empty gun full into the gargoyle face without effect, and with a lurch and a roll it had him in its grasp. As the giant arms closed crushingly about him, he abandoned all hope, but following his fighting instinct to the last, he drove his dagger hilt-deep in the shaggy belly.

But even as he struck, he felt a shudder run through the gigantic frame. The great arms fell away-and then he was hurled to the ground in the last death throe of the monster, and the thing was swaying, its face a deathmask. Dead on its feet, it crumpled, toppled to the ground, quivered and lay still. Not even a man-eating ape of Zambebwei could survive that close-range volley of mushrooming lead.

As the man staggered up, Constance rose and reeled into his arms, crying hysterically.

"It's all right now, Constance," he panted, crushing her to him. "The Zemba's dead; De Albor's dead; Ballville's dead; the negroes have run away. There's nothing to prevent us leaving now. The Moon of Zambebwei was the end for them. But it's the beginning of life for us."

Skull-Face

Chapter 1. The Face in the Mist

"We are no other than a moving row
Of Magic Shadow-shapes that come and go."
--Omar Khayyam

The horror first took concrete form amid that most unconcrete of all things--a hashish dream. I was off on a timeless, spaceless journey through the strange lands that belong to this state of being, a million miles away from earth and all things earthly; yet I became cognizant that something was reaching across the unknown voids--something that tore ruthlessly at the separating curtains of my illusions and intruded itself into my visions.

I did not exactly return to ordinary waking life, yet I was conscious of a seeing and a recognizing that was unpleasant and seemed out of keeping with the dream I was at that time enjoying. To one who has never known the delights of hashish, my explanation must seem chaotic and impossible. Still, I was aware of a rending of mists and then the Face intruded itself into my sight. I though at first it was merely a skull; then I saw that it was a hideous yellow instead of white, and was endowed with some horrid form of life. Eyes glimmered deep in the sockets and the jaws moved as if in speech. The body, except for the high, thin shoulders, was vague and indistinct, but the hands, which floated in the mists before and below the skull, were horribly vivid and filled me with crawling fears. They were like the hands of a mummy, long, lean and yellow, with knobby joints and cruel curving talons.

Then, to complete the vague horror which was swiftly taking possession of me, a voice spoke--imagine a man so long dead that his vocal organ had grown rusty and unaccustomed to speech. This was the thought which struck me and made my flesh crawl as I listened.

"A strong brute and one who might be useful somehow. See that he is given all the hashish he requires."

Then the face began to recede, even as I sensed that I was the subject of conversation, and the mists billowed and began to close again. Yet for a single instant a scene stood out with startling clarity. I gasped--or sought to. For over the high, strange shoulder of the apparition another face stood out clearly for an instant, as if the owner peered at me. Red lips, half-parted, long dark eyelashes, shading vivid eyes, a shimmery cloud of hair. Over the shoulder of Horror, breathtaking beauty for an instant looked at me.

Chapter 2. The Hashish Slave

*"Up from Earth's center through the Seventh Gate
I rose, and on the Throne of Saturn sate."*
--Omar Khayyam

My dream of the skull-face was borne over that usually uncrossable gap that lies between hashish enchantment and humdrum reality. I sat cross-legged on a mat in Yun Shatu's Temple of Dreams and gathered the fading forces of my decaying brain to the task of remembering events and faces.

This last dream was so entirely different from any I had ever had before, that my waning interest was roused to the point of inquiring as to its origin. When I first began to experiment with hashish, I sought to find a physical or psychic basis for the wild flights of illusion pertaining thereto, but of late I had been content to enjoy without seeking cause and effect.

Whence this unaccountable sensation of familiarity in regard to that vision? I took my throbbing head between my hands and laboriously sought a clue. A living dead man and a girl of rare beauty who had looked over his shoulder. Then I remembered.

Back in the fog of days and nights which veils a hashish addict's memory, my money had given out. It seemed years or possibly centuries, but my stagnant reason told me that it had probably been only a few days. At any rate, I had presented myself at Yun Shatu's sordid dive as usual and had been thrown out by the great Negro Hassim when it was learned I had no more money.

My universe crashing to pieces about me, and my nerves humming like taut piano wires for the vital need that was mine, I crouched in the gutter and gibbered bestially, till Hassim swaggered out and stilled my yammerings with a blow that felled me, half-stunned.

Then as I presently rose, staggeringly and with no thought save of the river which flowed with cool murmur so near me--as I rose, a light hand was laid like the touch of a rose on my arm. I turned with a frightened start, and stood spellbound before the vision of loveliness which met my gaze. Dark eyes limpid with pity surveyed me and the little hand on my ragged sleeve drew me toward the door of the Dream Temple. I shrank back, but a low voice, soft and musical, urged me, and filled with a trust that was strange, I shambled along with my beautiful guide.

At the door Hassim met us, cruel hands lifted and a dark scowl on his ape-like brow, but as I cowered there, expecting a blow, he halted before the girl's upraised hand and her word of command which had taken on an imperious note.

I did not understand what she said, but I saw dimly, as in a fog, that she gave the black man money, and she led me to a couch where she had me recline and arranged the cushions as if I were king of Egypt instead of a ragged, dirty renegade who lived only for hashish. Her slim hand was cool on my brow for a moment, and then she was gone and Yussef Ali came bearing the stuff for which my very soul shrieked--and soon I was wandering again through those strange and exotic countries that only a hashish slave knows.

Now as I sat on the mat and pondered the dream of the skull-face I wondered more. Since the unknown girl had led me back into the dive, I had come and gone as before, when I had plenty of money to pay Yun Shatu. Someone certainly was paying him for me, and while my subconscious mind had told me it was the girl, my rusty brain had failed to grasp the fact entirely, or to wonder why. What need of wondering? So someone paid and the vivid-hued dreams continued, what cared I? But now I wondered. For the girl who had protected me from Hassim and had brought the hashish for me was the same girl I had seen in the skull-face dream.

Through the soddenness of my degradation the lure of her struck like a knife piercing my heart and strangely revived the memories of the days when I was a man like other men--not yet a sullen, cringing slave of dreams. Far and dim they were, shimmery islands in the mist of years--and what a dark sea lay between!

I looked at my ragged sleeve and the dirty, claw-like hand protruding from it; I gazed through the hanging smoke which fogged the sordid room, at the low bunks along the wall whereon lay the blankly staring dreamers--slaves, like me, of hashish or of opium. I gazed at the slippered Chinamen gliding softly to and fro bearing pipes or roasting balls of concentrated purgatory over tiny flickering fires. I gazed at Hassim standing, arms folded, beside the door like a great statue of black basalt.

And I shuddered and hid my face in my hands because with the faint dawning of returning manhood, I knew that this last and most cruel dream was futile--I had crossed an ocean over which I could never return, had cut myself off from the world of normal men or women. Naught remained now but to drown this dream as I had drowned all my others--swiftly and with hope that I should soon attain that Ultimate Ocean which lies beyond all dreams.

So these fleeting moments of lucidity, of longing, that tear aside the veils of all dope slaves--unexplainable, without hope of attainment.

So I went back to my empty dreams, to my phantasmagoria of illusions; but sometimes, like a sword cleaving a mist, through the high lands and the low lands and seas of my visions floated, like half-forgotten music, the sheen of dark eyes and shimmery hair.

You ask how I, Stephen Costigan, American and a man of some attainments and culture, came to lie in a filthy dive of London's Limehouse? The answer is simple--no jaded debauchee, I, seeking new sensations in the mysteries of the Orient. I answer--Argonne! Heavens, what deeps and heights of horror lurk in that one word alone! Shell-shocked--shell-torn. Endless days and nights without end and roaring red hell over No Man's Land where I lay shot and bayoneted to shreds of gory flesh. My body recovered, how I know not; my mind never did.

And the leaping fires and shifting shadows in my tortured brain drove me down and down, along the stairs of degradation, uncaring until at last I found surcease in Yun Shatu's Temple of Dreams, where I slew my red dreams in other dreams--the dreams of hashish whereby a man may descend to the lower pits of the reddest hells or soar into those unnamable heights where the stars are diamond pinpoints beneath his feet.

Not the visions of the sot, the beast, were mine. I attained the unattainable, stood face to face with the unknown and in cosmic calmness knew the unguessable. And was content after a fashion, until the sight of burnished hair and scarlet lips swept away my dream-built universe and left me shuddering among its ruins.

Chapter 3. The Master of Doom

"And He that toss'd you down into the Field,
He knows about it all--He knows! He knows!"
--Omar Khayyam

A hand shook me roughly as I emerged languidly from my latest debauch.

"The Master wishes you! Up, swine!"

Hassim it was who shook me and who spoke.

"To Hell with the Master!" I answered, for I hated Hassim--and feared him.

"Up with you or you get no more hashish," was the brutal response, and I rose in trembling haste.

I followed the huge black man and he led the way to the rear of the building, stepping in and out among the wretched dreamers on the floor.

"Muster all hands on deck!" droned a sailor in a bunk. "All hands!"

Hassim flung open the door at the rear and motioned me to enter. I had never before passed through that door and had supposed it led into Yun Shatu's private quarters. But it was furnished only with a cot, a bronze idol of some sort before which incense burned, and a heavy table.

Hassim gave me a sinister glance and seized the table as if to spin it about. It turned as if it stood on a revolving platform and a section of the floor turned with it, revealing a hidden doorway in the floor. Steps led downward in the darkness.

Hassim lighted a candle and with a brusque gesture invited me to descend. I did so, with the sluggish obedience of the dope addict, and he followed, closing the door above us by means of an iron lever fastened to the underside of the floor. In the semi-darkness we went down the rickety steps, some nine or ten I should say, and then came upon a narrow corridor.

Here Hassim again took the lead, holding the candle high in front of him. I could scarcely see the sides of this cave-like passageway but knew that it was not wide. The flickering light showed it to be bare of any sort of furnishings save for a number of strange-looking chests which lined the walls--receptacles containing opium and other dope, I thought.

A continuous scurrying and the occasional glint of small red eyes haunted the shadows, betraying the presence of vast numbers of the great rats which infest the Thames waterfront of that section.

Then more steps loomed out of the dark in front of us as the corridor came to an abrupt end. Hassim led the way up and at the top knocked four times against what seemed the underside of a floor. A hidden door opened and a flood of soft, illusive light streamed through.

Hassim hustled me up roughly and I stood blinking in such a setting as I had never seen in my wildest flights of vision. I stood in a jungle of palm trees through which wriggled a million vivid-hued dragons! Then, as my startled eyes became accustomed to the light, I saw that I had not been suddenly transferred to some other planet, as I had at first thought. The palm trees were there, and the dragons, but the trees were artificial and stood in great pots and the dragons writhed across heavy tapestries which hid the walls.

The room itself was a monstrous affair--inhumanly large, it seemed to me. A thick smoke, yellowish and tropical in suggestion, seemed to hang over all, veiling the ceiling and baffling upward glances. This smoke, I saw, emanated from an altar in front of the wall to my left. I started. Through the saffron-billowing fog two eyes, hideously large and vivid, glittered at me. The vague outlines of some bestial idol took indistinct shape. I flung an uneasy glance about, marking the oriental divans and couches and the bizarre furnishings, and then my eyes halted and rested on a lacquer screen just in front of me.

I could not pierce it and no sound came from beyond it, yet I felt eyes searing into my consciousness through it, eyes that burned through my very soul. A strange aura of evil flowed from that strange screen with its weird carvings and unholy decorations.

Hassim salaamed profoundly before it and then, without speaking, stepped back and folded his arms, statue-like.

A voice suddenly broke the heavy and oppressive silence.

"You who are a swine, would you like to be a man again?"

I started. The tone was inhuman, cold--more, there was a suggestion of long disuse of the vocal organs--the voice I had heard in my dream!

"Yes," I replied, trance-like, "I would like to be a man again."

Silence ensued for a space; then the voice came again with a sinister whispering undertone at the back of its sound like bats flying through a cavern.

"I shall make you a man again because I am a friend to all broken men. Not for a price shall I do it, nor for gratitude. And I give you a sign to seal my promise and my vow. Thrust your hand through the screen."

At these strange and almost unintelligible words I stood perplexed, and then, as the unseen voice repeated the last command, I stepped forward and thrust my hand through a slit which opened silently in the screen. I felt my wrist seized in an iron grip and something seven times colder than ice touched the inside of my hand. Then my wrist was released, and drawing forth my hand I saw a strange symbol traced in blue close to the base of my thumb--a thing like a scorpion.

The voice spoke again in a sibilant language I did not understand, and Hassim stepped forward deferentially. He reached about the screen and then turned to me, holding a goblet of some amber-colored liquid which he proffered me with an ironical bow. I took it hesitatingly.

"Drink and fear not," said the unseen voice. "It is only an Egyptian wine with life-giving qualities."

So I raised the goblet and emptied it; the taste was not unpleasant, and even as I handed the beaker to Hassim again, I seemed to feel new life and vigor whip along my jaded veins.

"Remain at Yun Shatu's house," said the voice. "You will be given food and a bed until you are strong enough to work for yourself. You will use no hashish nor will you require any. Go!"

As in a daze, I followed Hassim back through the hidden door, down the steps, along the dark corridor and up through the other door that let us into the Temple of Dreams.

As we stepped from the rear chamber into the main room of the dreamers, I turned to the Negro wonderingly.

"Master? Master of what? Of Life?"

Hassim laughed, fiercely and sardonically.

"Master of Doom!"

Chapter 4. The Spider and the Fly

"There was the Door to which I found no Key;
There was the Veil through which I might not see."
--Omar Khayyam

I sat on Yun Shatu's cushions and pondered with a clearness of mind new and strange to me. As for that, all my sensations were new and strange. I felt as if I had wakened from a monstrously long sleep, and though my thoughts were sluggish, I felt as though the cobwebs which had dogged them for so long had been partly brushed away.

I drew my hand across my brow, noting how it trembled. I was weak and shaky and felt the stirrings of hunger--not for dope but for food. What had been in the draft I had quenched in the chamber of mystery? And why had the "Master" chosen me, out of all the other wretches of Yun Shatu's, for regeneration?

And who was this Master? Somehow the word sounded vaguely familiar--I sought laboriously to remember. Yes--I had heard it, lying half-waking in the bunks or on the floor--whispered sibilantly by Yun Shatu or by Hassim or by Yussef Ali, the Moor, muttered in their low-voiced conversations and mingled always with words I could not understand. Was not Yun Shatu, then, master of the Temple of Dreams? I had thought and the other addicts thought that the withered Chinaman held undisputed sway over this drab kingdom and that Hassim and Yussef Ali were his servants. And the four China boys who roasted opium with Yun Shatu and Yar Khan the Afghan and Santiago the Haitian and Ganra Singh, the renegade Sikh--all in the pay of Yun Shatu, we supposed--bound to the opium lord by bonds of gold or fear.

For Yun Shatu was a power in London's Chinatown and I had heard that his tentacles reached across the seas into high places of mighty and mysterious tongs. Was that Yun Shatu behind the lacquer screen?

No; I knew the Chinaman's voice and besides I had seen him puttering about in the front of the Temple just as I went through the back door.

Another thought came to me. Often, lying half-torpid, in the late hours of night or in the early grayness of dawn, I had seen men and women steal into the Temple, whose dress and bearing were strangely out of place and incongruous. Tall, erect men, often in evening dress, with their hats drawn low about their brows, and fine ladies, veiled, in silks and furs. Never two of them came together, but always they came separately and, hiding their features, hurried to the rear door, where they entered and presently came forth again, hours later sometimes. Knowing that the lust for dope finds resting-place in high positions sometimes, I had never wondered overmuch, supposing that these were wealthy men and women of society who had fallen victims to the craving, and that somewhere in the back of the building there was a private chamber for such. Yet now I wondered--sometimes these persons had remained only a few moments--was it always opium for which they came, or did they, too, traverse that strange corridor and converse with the One behind the screen?

My mind dallied with the idea of a great specialist to whom came all classes of people to find surcease from the dope habit. Yet it was strange that such a one should select a dope-joint from which to work--strange, too, that the owner of that house should apparently look on him with so much reverence.

I gave it up as my head began to hurt with the unwonted effort of thinking, and shouted for food. Yussef Ali brought it to me on a tray, with a promptness which was surprizing. More, he salaamed as he departed, leaving me to ruminate on the strange shift of my status in the Temple of Dreams.

I ate, wondering what the One of the screen wanted with me. Not for an instant did I suppose that his actions had been prompted by the reasons he pretended; the life of the underworld had taught me that none of its denizens leaned toward philanthropy. And underworld the chamber of mystery had been, in spite of its elaborate and bizarre nature. And where could it be located? How far had I walked along the corridor? I shrugged my shoulders, wondering if it were not all a hashish-induced dream; then my eye fell upon my hand--and the scorpion traced thereon.

"Muster all hands!" droned the sailor in the bunk. "All hands!"

To tell in detail of the next few days would be boresome to any who have not tasted the dire slavery of dope. I waited for the craving to strike me again--waited with sure sardonic hopelessness. All day, all night--another day--then the miracle was forced upon my doubting brain. Contrary to all theories and supposed facts of science and common sense the craving had left me as suddenly and completely as a bad dream! At first I could not credit my senses but believed myself to be still in the grip of a dope nightmare. But it was true. From the time I quaffed the goblet in the room of mystery, I felt not the slightest desire for the stuff which had been life itself to me. This, I felt vaguely, was somehow unholy and certainly opposed to all rules of nature. If the dread being behind the screen had discovered the secret of breaking hashish's terrible power, what other monstrous secrets had he discovered and what unthinkable dominance was his? The suggestion of evil crawled serpent-like through my mind.

I remained at Yun Shatu's house, lounging in a bunk or on cushions spread upon the floor, eating and drinking at will, but now that I was becoming a normal man again, the atmosphere became most revolting to me and the sight of the wretches writhing in their dreams reminded me unpleasantly of what I myself had been, and it repelled, nauseated me.

So one day, when no one was watching me, I rose and went out on the street and walked along the waterfront. The air, burdened though it was with smoke and foul scents, filled my lungs with strange freshness and aroused new vigor in what had once been a powerful frame. I took new interest in the sounds of men living and working, and the sight of a vessel being unloaded at one of the wharfs actually thrilled me. The force of longshoremen was short, and presently I found myself heaving and lifting and carrying, and though the sweat coursed down my brow and my limbs trembled at the effort, I exulted in the thought that at last I was able to labor for myself again, no matter how low or drab the work might be.

As I returned to the door of Yun Shatu's that evening--hideously weary but with the renewed feeling of manhood that comes of honest toil--Hassim met me at the door.

"You been where?" he demanded roughly.

"I've been working on the docks," I answered shortly.

"You don't need to work on docks," he snarled. "The Master got work for you."

He led the way, and again I traversed the dark stairs and the corridor under the earth. This time my faculties were alert and I decided that the passageway could not be over thirty or forty feet in length. Again I stood before the lacquer screen and again I heard the inhuman voice of living death.

"I can give you work," said the voice. "Are you willing to work for me?"

I quickly assented. After all, in spite of the fear which the voice inspired, I was deeply indebted to the owner.

"Good. Take these."

As I started toward the screen a sharp command halted me and Hassim stepped forward and reaching behind took what was offered. This was a bundle of pictures and papers, apparently.

"Study these," said the One behind the screen, "and learn all you can about the man portrayed thereby. Yun Shatu will give you money; buy yourself such clothes as seamen wear and take a room at the front of the Temple. At the end of two days, Hassim will bring you to me again. Go!"

The last impression I had, as the hidden door closed above me, was that the eyes of the idol, blinking through the everlasting smoke, leered mockingly at me.

The front of the Temple of Dreams consisted of rooms for rent, masking the true purpose of the building under the guise of a waterfront boarding house. The police had made several visits to Yun Shatu but had never got any incriminating evidence against him.

So in one of these rooms I took up my abode and set to work studying the material given me.

The pictures were all of one man, a large man, not unlike me in build and general facial outline, except that he wore a heavy beard and was inclined to blondness whereas I am dark. The name, as written on the accompanying papers, was Major Fairlan Morley, special commissioner to Natal and the Transvaal. This office and title were new to me and I wondered at the connection between an African commissioner and an opium house on the Thames waterfront.

The papers consisted of extensive data evidently copied from authentic sources and all dealing with Major Morley, and a number of private documents considerably illuminating on the major's private life.

An exhaustive description was given of the man's personal appearance and habits, some of which seemed very trivial to me. I wondered what the purpose could be, and how the One behind the screen had come in possession of papers of such intimate nature.

I could find no clue in answer to this question but bent all my energies to the task set out for me. I owed a deep debt of gratitude to the unknown man who required this of me and I was determined to repay him to the best of my ability. Nothing, at this time, suggested a snare to me.

Chapter 5. The Man on the Couch

"What dam of lances sent thee forth to jest at dawn with Death?"
--Kipling

At the expiration of two days, Hassim beckoned me as I stood in the opium room. I advanced with a springy, resilient tread, secure in the confidence that I had culled the Morley papers of all their worth. I was a new man; my mental swiftness and physical readiness surprized me--sometimes it seemed unnatural.

Hassim eyed me through narrowed lids and motioned me to follow, as usual. As we crossed the room, my gaze fell upon a man who lay on a couch close to the wall, smoking opium. There was nothing at all suspicious about his ragged, unkempt clothes, his dirty, bearded face or the blank stare, but my eyes, sharpened to an abnormal point, seemed to sense a certain incongruity in the clean-cut limbs which not even the slouchy garments could efface.

Hassim spoke impatiently and I turned away. We entered the rear room, and as he shut the door and turned to the table, it moved of itself and a figure bulked up through the hidden doorway. The Sikh, Ganra Singh, a lean sinister-eyed giant, emerged and proceeded to the door opening into the opium room, where he halted until we should have descended and closed the secret doorway.

Again I stood amid the billowing yellow smoke and listened to the hidden voice.

"Do you think you know enough about Major Morley to impersonate him successfully?"

Startled, I answered, "No doubt I could, unless I met someone who was intimate with him."

"I will take care of that. Follow me closely. Tomorrow you sail on the first boat for Calais. There you will meet an agent of mine who will accost you the instant you step upon the wharfs, and give you further instructions. You will sail second class and avoid all conversation with strangers or anyone. Take the papers with you. The agent will aid you in making up and your masquerade will start in Calais. That is all. Go!"

I departed, my wonder growing. All this rigmarole evidently had a meaning, but one which I could not fathom. Back in the opium room Hassim bade me be seated on some cushions to await his return. To my question he snarled that he was going forth as he had been ordered, to buy me a ticket on the Channel boat. He departed and I sat down, leaning my back against the wall. As I ruminated, it seemed suddenly that eyes were fixed on me so intensely as to disturb my sub-mind. I glanced up quickly but no one seemed to be looking at me. The smoke drifted through the hot atmosphere as usual; Yussef Ali and the Chinese glided back and forth tending to the wants of the sleepers.

Suddenly the door to the rear room opened and a strange and hideous figure came haltingly out. Not all of those who found entrance to Yun Shatu's back room were aristocrats and society members. This was one of the exceptions, and one whom I remembered as having often entered and emerged therefrom. A tall, gaunt figure, shapeless and ragged wrappings and nondescript garments, face entirely hidden. Better that the face be hidden, I thought, for without doubt the wrapping concealed a grisly sight. The man was a leper, who had somehow managed to escape the attention of the public guardians and who was occasionally seen haunting the lower and more mysterious regions of East End--a mystery even to the lowest denizens of Limehouse.

Suddenly my supersensitive mind was aware of a swift tension in the air. The leper hobbled out the door, closed it behind him. My eyes instinctively sought the couch whereon lay the man who had aroused my suspicions earlier in the day. I could have sworn that cold steely eyes glared menacingly before they flickered shut. I crossed to the couch in one stride and bent over the prostrate man. Something about his face seemed unnatural--a healthy bronze seemed to underlie the pallor of complexion.

"Yun Shatu!" I shouted. "A spy is in the house!"

Things happened then with bewildering speed. The man on the couch with one tigerish movement leaped erect and a revolver gleamed in his hand. One sinewy arm flung me aside as I sought to grapple with him and a sharp decisive voice sounded over the babble which broke forth.

"You there! Halt! Halt!"

The pistol in the stranger's hand was leveled at the leper, who was making for the door in long strides!

All about was confusion; Yun Shatu was shrieking volubly in Chinese and the four China boys and Yussef Ali were rushing in from all sides, knives glittering in their hands.

All this I saw with unnatural clearness even as I marked the stranger's face. As the fleeing leper gave no evidence of halting, I saw the eyes harden to steely points of determination, sighting along the pistol barrel--the features set with the grim purpose of the slayer. The leper was almost to the outer door, but death would strike him down ere he could reach it.

And then, just as the finger of the stranger tightened on the trigger, I hurled myself forward and my right fist crashed against his chin. He went down as though struck by a trip-hammer, the revolver exploding harmlessly in the air.

In that instant, with the blinding flare of light that sometimes comes to one, I knew that the leper was none other than the Man Behind the Screen!

I bent over the fallen man, who though not entirely senseless had been rendered temporarily helpless by that terrific blow. He was struggling dazedly to rise but I shoved him roughly down again and seizing the false beard he wore, tore it away. A lean bronzed face was revealed, the strong lines of which not even the artificial dirt and greasepaint could alter.

Yussef Ali leaned above him now, dagger in hand, eyes slits of murder. The brown sinewy hand went up--I caught the wrist.

"Not so fast, you black devil! What are you about to do?"

"This is John Gordon," he hissed, "the Master's greatest foe! He must die, curse you!"

John Gordon! The name was familiar somehow, and yet I did not seem to connect it with the London police nor account for the man's presence in Yun Shatu's dope-joint. However, on one point I was determined.

"You don't kill him, at any rate. Up with you!" This last to Gordon, who with my aid staggered up, still very dizzy.

"That punch would have dropped a bull," I said in wonderment; "I didn't know I had it in me."

The false leper had vanished. Yun Shatu stood gazing at me as immobile as an idol, hands in his wide sleeves, and Yussef Ali stood back, muttering murderously and thumbing his dagger edge, as I led

Gordon out of the opium room and through the innocent-appearing bar which lay between that room and the street.

Out in the street I said to him: "I have no idea as to who you are or what you are doing here, but you see what an unhealthful place it is for you. Hereafter be advised by me and stay away."

His only answer was a searching glance, and then be turned and walked swiftly though somewhat unsteadily up the street.

Chapter 6. The Dream Girl

"I have reached these lands but newly
From an ultimate dim Thule."
--Poe

Outside my room sounded a light footstep. The doorknob turned cautiously and slowly; the door opened. I sprang erect with a gasp. Red lips, half-parted, dark eyes like limpid seas of wonder, a mass of shimmering hair--framed in my drab doorway stood the girl of my dreams!

She entered, and half-turning with a sinuous motion, closed the door. I sprang forward, my hands outstretched, then halted as she put a finger to her lips.

"You must not talk loudly," she almost whispered. "He did not say I could not come; yet--"

Her voice was soft and musical, with just a touch of foreign accent which I found delightful. As for the girl herself, every intonation, every movement proclaimed the Orient. She was a fragrant breath from the East. From her night-black hair, piled high above her alabaster forehead, to her little feet, encased in high-heeled pointed slippers, she portrayed the highest ideal of Asiatic loveliness--an effect which was heightened rather than lessened by the English blouse and skirt which she wore.

"You are beautiful!" I said dazedly. "Who are you?"

"I am Zuleika," she answered with a shy smile. "I--I am glad you like me. I am glad you no longer dream hashish dreams."

Strange that so small a thing should set my heart to leaping wildly!

"I owe it all to you, Zuleika," I said huskily. "Had not I dreamed of you every hour since you first lifted me from the gutter, I had lacked the power of even hoping to be freed from my curse."

She blushed prettily and intertwined her white fingers as if in nervousness.

"You leave England tomorrow?" she said suddenly.

"Yes. Hassim has not returned with my ticket--" I hesitated suddenly, remembering the command of silence.

"Yes, I know, I know!" she whispered swiftly, her eyes widening. "And John Gordon has been here! He saw you!"

"Yes!"

She came close to me with a quick lithe movement.

"You are to impersonate some man! Listen, while you are doing this, you must not ever let Gordon see you! He would know you, no matter what your disguise! He is a terrible man!"

"I don't understand," I said, completely bewildered. "How did the Master break me of my hashish craving? Who is this Gordon and why did he come here? Why does the Master go disguised as a leper--and who is he? Above all, why am I to impersonate a man I never saw or heard of?"

"I cannot--I dare not tell you!" she whispered, her face paling. "I--"

Somewhere in the house sounded the faint tones of a Chinese gong. The girl started like a frightened gazelle.

"I must go! *He* summons me!"

She opened the door, darted through, halted a moment to electrify me with her passionate exclamation: "Oh, be careful, be very careful, sahib!"

Then she was gone.

Chapter 7. The Man of the Skull

"What the hammer? What the chain?
In what furnace was thy brain?
What the anvil? What dread grasp
Dare its deadly terrors clasp?"
--Blake

A while after my beautiful and mysterious visitor had left, I sat in meditation. I believed that I had at last stumbled onto an explanation of a part of the enigma, at any rate. This was the conclusion I had reached: Yun Shatu, the opium lord, was simply the agent or servant of some organization or individual whose work was on a far larger scale than merely supplying dope addicts in the Temple of Dreams. This man or these men needed co-workers among all classes of people; in other words, I was being let in with a group of opium smugglers on a gigantic scale. Gordon no doubt had been investigating the case, and his presence alone showed that it was no ordinary one, for I knew that he held a high position with the English government, though just what, I did not know.

Opium or not, I determined to carry out my obligation to the Master. My moral sense had been blunted by the dark ways I had traveled, and the thought of despicable crime did not enter my head. I was indeed hardened. More, the mere debt of gratitude was increased a thousand-fold by the thought of the girl. To the Master I owed it that I was able to stand up on my feet and look into her clear eyes as a man should. So if he wished my services as a smuggler of dope, he should have them. No doubt I was to impersonate some man so high in governmental esteem that the usual actions of the customs officers would be deemed unnecessary; was I to bring some rare dream-producer into England?

These thoughts were in my mind as I went downstairs, but ever back of them hovered other and more alluring suppositions--what was the reason for the girl, here in this vile dive--a rose in a garbage-heap-- and who was she?

As I entered the outer bar, Hassim came in, his brows set in a dark scowl of anger, and, I believed, fear. He carried a newspaper in his hand, folded.

"I told you to wait in opium room," he snarled.

"You were gone so long that I went up to my room. Have you the ticket?"

He merely grunted and pushed on past me into the opium room, and standing at the door I saw him cross the floor and disappear into the rear room. I stood there, my bewilderment increasing. For as Hassim had brushed past me, I had noted an item on the face of the paper, against which his black thumb was tightly pressed as if to mark that special column of news.

And with the unnatural celerity of action and judgment which seemed to be mine those days, I had in that fleeting instant read:

African Special Commissioner Found Murdered!

The body of Major Fairlan Morley was yesterday discovered in a rotting ship's hold at Bordeaux...

No more I saw of the details, but that alone was enough to make me think! The affair seemed to be taking on an ugly aspect. Yet--

Another day passed. To my inquiries, Hassim snarled that the plans had been changed and I was not to go to France. Then, late in the evening, he came to bid me once more to the room of mystery.

I stood before the lacquer screen, the yellow smoke acrid in my nostrils, the woven dragons writhing along the tapestries, the palm trees rearing thick and oppressive.

"A change has come in our plans," said the hidden voice. "You will not sail as was decided before. But I have other work that you may do. Mayhap this will be more to your type of usefulness, for I admit you have somewhat disappointed me in regard to subtlety. You interfered the other day in such manner as will no doubt cause me great inconvenience in the future."

I said nothing, but a feeling of resentment began to stir in me.

"Even after the assurance of one of my most trusted servants," the toneless voice continued, with no mark of any emotion save a slightly rising note, "you insisted on releasing my most deadly enemy. Be more circumspect in the future."

"I saved your life!" I said angrily.

73

"And for that reason alone I overlook your mistake--this time!"

A slow fury suddenly surged up in me.

"This time! Make the best of it this time, for I assure you there will be no next time. I owe you a greater debt than I can ever hope to pay, but that does not make me your slave. I have saved your life--the debt is as near paid as a man can pay it. Go your way and I go mine!"

A low, hideous laugh answered me, like a reptilian hiss.

"You fool! You will pay with your whole life's toil! You say you are not my slave? I say you are--just as black Hassim there beside you is my slave--just as the girl Zuleika is my slave, who has bewitched you with her beauty."

These words sent a wave of hot blood to my brain and I was conscious of a flood of fury which completely engulfed my reason for a second. Just as all my moods and senses seemed sharpened and exaggerated those days, so now this burst of rage transcended every moment of anger I had ever had before.

"Hell's fiends!" I shrieked. "You devil--who are you and what is your hold on me? I'll see you or die!"

Hassim sprang at me, but I hurled him backward and with one stride reached the screen and flung it aside with an incredible effort of strength. Then I shrank back, hands outflung, shrieking. A tall, gaunt figure stood before me, a figure arrayed grotesquely in a silk brocaded gown which fell to the floor.

From the sleeves of this gown protruded hands which filled me with crawling horror--long, predatory hands, with thin bony fingers and curved talons--withered skin of a parchment brownish-yellow, like the hands of a man long dead.

The hands--but, oh God, the face! A skull to which no vestige of flesh seemed to remain but on which taut brownish-yellow skin grew fast, etching out every detail of that terrible death's-head. The forehead was high and in a way magnificent, but the head was curiously narrow through the temples, and from under penthouse brows great eyes glimmered like pools of yellow fire. The nose was high-bridged and very thin; the mouth was a mere colorless gash between thin, cruel lips. A long, bony neck supported this frightful vision and completed the effect of a reptilian demon from some medieval hell.

I was face to face with the skull-faced man of my dreams!

Chapter 8. Black Wisdom

"By thought a crawling ruin,
By life a leaping mire.
By a broken heart in the breast of the world
And the end of the world's desire."
--Chesterton

The terrible spectacle drove for the instant all thought of rebellion from my mind. My very blood froze in my veins and I stood motionless. I heard Hassim laugh grimly behind me. The eyes in the cadaverous face blazed fiendishly at me and I blanched from the concentrated satanic fury in them.

Then the horror laughed sibilantly.

"I do you a great honor, Mr. Costigan; among a very few, even of my own servants, you may say that you saw my face and lived. I think you will be more useful to me living than dead."

I was silent, completely unnerved. It was difficult to believe that this man lived, for his appearance certainly belied the thought. He seemed horribly like a mummy. Yet his lips moved when he spoke and his eyes flamed with hideous life.

"You will do as I say," he said abruptly, and his voice had taken on a note of command. "You doubtless know, or know of, Sir Haldred Frenton?"

"Yes."

Every man of culture in Europe and America was familiar with the travel books of Sir Haldred Frenton, author and soldier of fortune.

"You will go to Sir Haldred's estate tonight--"

"Yes?"

"And kill him!"

I staggered, literally. This order was incredible--unspeakable! I had sunk low, low enough to smuggle opium, but to deliberately murder a man I had never seen, a man noted for his kindly deeds! That was too monstrous even to contemplate.

"You do not refuse?"

The tone was as loathly and as mocking as the hiss of a serpent.

"Refuse?" I screamed, finding my voice at last. "Refuse? You incarnate devil! Of course I refuse! You--"

Something in the cold assurance of his manner halted me--froze me into apprehensive silence.

"You fool!" he said calmly. "I broke the hashish chains--do you know how? Four minutes from now you will know and curse the day you were born! Have you not thought it strange, the swiftness of brain, the resilience of body--the brain that should be rusty and slow, the body that should be weak and sluggish from years of abuse? That blow that felled John Gordon--have you not wondered at its might? The ease with which you mastered Major Morley's records--have you not wondered at that? You fool, you are bound to me by chains of steel and blood and fire! I have kept you alive and sane--I alone. Each day the life-saving elixir has been given you in your wine. You could not live and keep your reason without it. And I and only I know its secret!"

He glanced at a queer timepiece which stood on a table at his elbow.

"This time I had Yun Shatu leave the elixir out--I anticipated rebellion. The time is near--ha, it strikes!"

Something else he said, but I did not hear. I did not see, nor did I feel in the human sense of the word. I was writhing at his feet, screaming and gibbering in the flames of such hells as men have never dreamed of.

Aye, I knew now! He had simply given me a dope so much stronger that it drowned the hashish. My unnatural ability was explainable now--I had simply been acting under the stimulus of something which combined all the hells in its makeup, which stimulated, something like heroin, but whose effect was unnoticed by the victim. What it was, I had no idea, nor did I believe anyone knew save that hellish being who stood watching me with grim amusement. But it had held my brain together, instilling into my system a need for it, and now my frightful craving tore my soul asunder.

Never, in my moments of worst shell-shock or my moments of hashish-craving, have I ever experienced anything like that. I burned with the heat of a thousand hells and froze with an iciness that was colder than any ice, a hundred times. I swept down to the deepest pits of torture and up to the highest crags of torment--a million yelling devils hemmed me in, shrieking and stabbing. Bone by bone, vein by vein, cell by cell I felt my body disintegrate and fly in bloody atoms all over the universe--and each separate cell was an entire system of quivering, screaming nerves. And they gathered from far voids and reunited with a greater torment.

Through the fiery bloody mists I heard my own voice screaming, a monotonous yammering. Then with distended eyes I saw a golden goblet, held by a claw-like hand, swim into view--a goblet filled with an amber liquid.

With a bestial screech, I seized it with both hands, being dimly aware that the metal stem gave beneath my fingers, and brought the brim to my lips. I drank in frenzied haste, the liquid slopping down onto my breast.

Chapter 9. Kathulos of Egypt

"Night shall be thrice night over you,
And Heaven an iron cope."
--Chesterton

The Skull-faced One stood watching me critically as I sat panting on a couch, completely exhausted. He held in his hand the goblet and surveyed the golden stem, which was crushed out of all shape. This my maniac fingers had done in the instant of drinking.

"Superhuman strength, even for a man in your condition," he said with a sort of creaky pedantry. "I doubt if even Hassim here could equal it. Are you ready for your instructions now?"

I nodded, wordless. Already the hellish strength of the elixir was flowing through my veins, renewing my burnt-out force. I wondered how long a man could live as I lived being constantly burned out and artificially rebuilt.

"You will be given a disguise and will go alone to the Frenton estate. No one suspects any design against Sir Haldred and your entrance into the estate and the house itself should be a matter of comparative ease. You will not don the disguise--which will be of unique nature-- until you are ready to enter the estate. You will then proceed to Sir Haldred's room and kill him, breaking his neck with your bare hands-- this is essential--"

The voice droned on, giving the ghastly orders in a frightfully casual and matter-of-fact way. The cold sweat beaded my brow.

"You will then leave the estate, taking care to leave the imprint of your hand somewhere plainly visible, and the automobile, which will be waiting for you at some safe place nearby, will bring you back here, you having first removed the disguise. I have, in case of complications, any amount of men who will swear that you spent the entire night in the Temple of Dreams and never left it. But here must be no detection! Go warily and perform your task surely, for you know the alternative."

I did not return to the opium house but was taken through winding corridors, hung with heavy tapestries, to a small room containing only an oriental couch. Hassim gave me to understand that I was to remain here until after nightfall and then left me. The door was closed but I made no effort to discover if it was locked. The Skull-faced Master held me with stronger shackles than locks and bolts.

Seated upon the couch in the bizarre setting of a chamber which might have been a room in an Indian zenana, I faced fact squarely and fought out my battle. There was still in me some trace of manhood left--more than the fiend had reckoned, and added to this were black despair and desperation. I chose and determined on my only course.

Suddenly the door opened softly. Some intuition told me whom to expect, nor was I disappointed. Zuleika stood, a glorious vision before me--a vision which mocked me, made blacker my despair and yet thrilled me with wild yearning and reasonless joy.

She bore a tray of food which she set beside me, and then she seated herself on the couch, her large eyes fixed upon my face. A flower in a serpent den she was, and the beauty of her took hold of my heart.

"Steephen!" she whispered, and I thrilled as she spoke my name for the first time.

Her luminous eyes suddenly shone with tears and she laid her little hand on my arm. I seized it in both my rough hands.

"They have set you a task which you fear and hate!" she faltered.

"Aye," I almost laughed, "but I'll fool them yet! Zuleika, tell me-- what is the meaning of all this?"

She glanced fearfully around her.

"I do not know all"--she hesitated--"your plight is all my fault but I--I hoped--Steephen, I have watched you every time you came to Yun Shatu's for months. You did not see me but I saw you, and I saw in you, not the broken sot your rags proclaimed, but a wounded soul, a soul bruised terribly on the ramparts of life. And from my heart I pitied you. Then when Hassim abused you that day"--again tears started to her eyes--"I could not bear it and I knew how you suffered for want of hashish. So I paid Yun Shatu, and going to the Master I--I--oh, you will hate me for this!" she sobbed.

"No--no--never--"

"I told him that you were a man who might be of use to him and begged him to have Yun Shatu supply you with what you needed. He had already noticed you, for his is the eye of the slaver and all the world is his slave market! So he bade Yun Shatu do as I asked; and now--better if you had remained as you were, my friend."

"No! No!" I exclaimed. "I have known a few days of regeneration, even if it was false! I have stood before you as a man, and that is worth all else!"

And all that I felt for her must have looked forth from my eyes, for she dropped hers and flushed. Ask me not how love comes to a man; but I knew that I loved Zuleika--had loved this mysterious oriental girl since first I saw her--and somehow I felt that she, in a measure, returned my affection. This realization made blacker and more barren the road I had chosen; yet--for pure love must ever strengthen a man--it nerved me to what I must do.

"Zuleika," I said, speaking hurriedly, "time flies and there are things I must learn; tell me--who are you and why do you remain in this den of Hades?"

"I am Zuleika--that is all I know. I am Circassian by blood and birth; when I was very little I was captured in a Turkish raid and raised in a Stamboul harem; while I was yet too young to marry, my master gave me as a present to--to *Him*."

"And who is he--this skull-faced man?"

"He is Kathulos of Egypt--that is all I know. My master."

"An Egyptian? Then what is he doing in London--why all this mystery?"

She intertwined her fingers nervously.

"Steephen, please speak lower; always there is someone listening everywhere. I do not know who the Master is or why he is here or why he does these things. I swear by Allah! If I knew I would tell you. Sometimes distinguished-looking men come here to the room where the Master receives them--not the room where you saw him--and he makes me dance before them and afterward flirt with them a little. And always I must repeat exactly what they say to me. That is what I must always do--in Turkey, in the Barbary States, in Egypt, in France and in England. The Master taught me French and English and educated me in many ways himself. He is the greatest sorcerer in all the world and knows all ancient magic and everything."

"Zuleika," I said, "my race is soon run, but let me get you out of this--come with me and I swear I'll get you away from this fiend!"

She shuddered and hid her face.

"No, no, I cannot!"

"Zuleika," I asked gently, "what hold has he over you, child--dope also?"

"No, no!" she whimpered. "I do not know--I do not know--but I cannot--I never can escape him!"

I sat, baffled for a few moments; then I asked, "Zuleika, where are we right now?"

"This building is a deserted storehouse back of the Temple of Silence."

"I thought so. What is in the chests in the tunnel?"

"I do not know."

Then suddenly she began weeping softly. "You too, a slave, like me--you who are so strong and kind--oh Steephen, I cannot bear it!"

I smiled. "Lean closer, Zuleika, and I will tell you how I am going to fool this Kathulos."

She glanced apprehensively at the door.

"You must speak low. I will lie in your arms and while you pretend to caress me, whisper your words to me."

She glided into my embrace, and there on the dragon-worked couch in that house of horror I first knew the glory of Zuleika's slender form nestling in my arms--of Zuleika's soft cheek pressing my breast. The fragrance of her was in my nostrils, her hair in my eyes, and my senses reeled; then with my lips hidden by her silky hair I whispered, swiftly:

"I am going first to warn Sir Haldred Frenton--then to find John Gordon and tell him of this den. I will lead the police here and you must watch closely and be ready to hide from *Him* --until we can break through and kill or capture him. Then you will be free."

"But you!" she gasped, paling. "You must have the elixir, and only he--"

"I have a way of outdoing him, child," I answered.

She went pitifully white and her woman's intuition sprang at the right conclusion.

"You are going to kill yourself!"

And much as it hurt me to see her emotion, I yet felt a torturing thrill that she should feel so on my account. Her arms tightened about my neck.

"Don't, Steephen!" she begged. "It is better to live, even--"

"No, not at that price. Better to go out clean while I have the manhood left."

She stared at me wildly for an instant; then, pressing her red lips suddenly to mine, she sprang up and fled from the room. Strange, strange are the ways of love. Two stranded ships on the shores of life, we had drifted inevitably together, and though no word of love had passed between us, we knew each other's heart--through grime and rags, and through accouterments of the slave, we knew each other's heart and from the first loved as naturally and as purely as it was intended from the beginning of Time.

The beginning of life now and the end for me, for as soon as I had completed my task, ere I felt again the torments of my curse, love and life and beauty and torture should be blotted out together in the stark finality of a pistol ball scattering my rotting brain. Better a clean death than--

The door opened again and Yussef Ali entered.

"The hour arrives for departure," he said briefly. "Rise and follow."

I had no idea, of course, as to the time. No window opened from the room I occupied--I had seen no outer window whatever. The rooms were lighted by tapers in censers swinging from the ceiling. As I rose the slim young Moor slanted a sinister glance in my direction.

"This lies between you and me," he said sibilantly. "Servants of the same Master we--but this concerns ourselves alone. Keep your distance from Zuleika--the Master has promised her to me in the days of the empire."

My eyes narrowed to slits as I looked into the frowning, handsome face of the Oriental, and such hate surged up in me as I have seldom known. My fingers involuntarily opened and closed, and the Moor, marking the action, stepped back, hand in his girdle.

"Not now--there is work for us both--later perhaps." Then in a sudden cold gust of hatred, "Swine! Ape-man! When the Master is finished with you I shall quench my dagger in your heart!"

I laughed grimly.

"Make it soon, desert-snake, or I'll crush your spine between my hands."

Chapter 10. The Dark House

"Against all man-made shackles and a man-made hell--
Alone--at last--unaided--I rebel!"
--Mundy

I followed Yussef Ali along the winding hallways, down the steps--
Kathulos was not in the idol room--and along the tunnel, then through
the rooms of the Temple of Dreams and out into the street, where the
street lamps gleamed drearily through the fogs and a slight drizzle.
Across the street stood an automobile, curtains closely drawn.

"That is yours," said Hassim, who had joined us. "Saunter across
natural-like. Don't act suspicious. The place may be watched. The
driver knows what to do."

Then he and Yussef Ali drifted back into the bar and I took a single
step toward the curb.

"Steephen!"

A voice that made my heart leap spoke my name! A white hand
beckoned from the shadows of a doorway. I stepped quickly there.

"Zuleika!"

"Shhh!"

She clutched my arm, slipped something into my hand; I made out
vaguely a small flask of gold.

"Hide this, quick!" came her urgent whisper. "Don't come back but
go away and hide. This is full of elixir--I will try to get you some more
before that is all gone. You must find a way of communicating with
me."

"Yes, but how did you get this?" I asked amazedly.

"I stole it from the Master! Now please, I must go before he misses
me."

And she sprang back into the doorway and vanished. I stood undecided. I was sure that she had risked nothing less than her life in doing

this and I was torn by the fear of what Kathulos might do to her, were the theft discovered. But to return to the house of mystery would certainly invite suspicion, and I might carry out my plan and strike back before the Skull-faced One learned of his slave's duplicity.

So I crossed the street to the waiting automobile. The driver was a Negro whom I had never seen before, a lanky man of medium height. I stared hard at him, wondering how much he had seen. He gave no evidence of having seen anything, and I decided that even if he had noticed me step back into the shadows he could not have seen what passed there nor have been able to recognize the girl.

He merely nodded as I climbed in the back seat, and a moment later we were speeding away down the deserted and fog-haunted streets. A bundle beside me I concluded to be the disguise mentioned by the Egyptian.

To recapture the sensations I experienced as I rode through the rainy, misty night would be impossible. I felt as if I were already dead and the bare and dreary streets about me were the roads of death over which my ghost had been doomed to roam forever. A torturing joy was in my heart, and bleak despair--the despair of a doomed man. Not that death itself was so repellent--a dope victim dies too many deaths to shrink from the last--but it was hard to go out just as love had entered my barren life. And I was still young.

A sardonic smile crossed my lips--they were young, too, the men who died beside me in No Man's Land. I drew back my sleeve and clenched my fists, tensing my muscles. There was no surplus weight on my frame, and much of the firm flesh had wasted away, but the cords of the great biceps still stood out like knots of iron, seeming to indicate massive strength. But I knew my might was false, that in reality I was a broken hulk of a man, animated only by the artificial fire of the elixir, without which a frail girl might topple me over.

The automobile came to a halt among some trees. We were on the outskirts of an exclusive suburb and the hour was past midnight. Through the trees I saw a large house looming darkly against the distant flares of nighttime London.

"This is where I wait," said the Negro. "No one can see the automobile from the road or from the house."

Holding a match so that its light could not be detected outside the car, I examined the "disguise" and was hard put to restrain an insane laugh. The disguise was the complete hide of a gorilla! Gathering the bundle under my arm I trudged toward the wall which surrounded the Frenton estate. A few steps and the trees where the Negro hid with the car merged into one dark mass. I did not believe he could see me, but for safety's sake I made, not for the high iron gate at the front, but for the wall at the side where there was no gate.

No light showed in the house. Sir Haldred was a bachelor and I was sure that the servants were all in bed long ago. I negotiated the wall with ease and stole across the dark lawn to a side door, still carrying the grisly "disguise" under my arm. The door was locked, as I had anticipated, and I did not wish to arouse anyone until I was safely in the house, where the sound of voices would not carry to one who might have followed me. I took hold of the knob with both hands, and, exerting slowly the inhuman strength that was mine, began to twist. The shaft turned in my hands and the lock within shattered suddenly, with a noise that was like the crash of a cannon in the stillness. An instant more and I was inside and had closed the door behind me.

I took a single stride in the darkness in the direction I believed the stair to be, then halted as a beam of light flashed into my face. At the side of the beam I caught the glimmer of a pistol muzzle. Beyond a lean shadowy face floated.

"Stand where you are and put up your hands!"

I lifted my hands, allowing the bundle to slip to the floor. I had heard that voice only once but I recognized it--knew instantly that the man who held that light was John Gordon.

"How many are with you?"

His voice was sharp, commanding.

"I am alone," I answered. "Take me into a room where a light cannot be seen from the outside and I'll tell you some things you want to know."

He was silent; then, bidding me take up the bundle I had dropped, he stepped to one side and motioned me to precede him into the next room. There he directed me to a stairway and at the top landing opened a door and switched on lights.

I found myself in a room whose curtains were closely drawn. During this journey Gordon's alertness had not relaxed, and now he stood, still covering me with his revolver. Clad in conventional garments, he stood revealed a tall, leanly but powerfully built man, taller than I but not so heavy--with steel-gray eyes and clean-cut features. Something about the man attracted me, even as I noted a bruise on his jawbone where my fist had struck in our last meeting.

"I cannot believe," he said crisply, "that this apparent clumsiness and lack of subtlety is real. Doubtless you have your own reasons for wishing me to be in a secluded room at this time, but Sir Haldred is efficiently protected even now. Stand still."

Muzzle pressed against my chest, he ran his hand over my garments for concealed weapons, seeming slightly surprized when he found none.

"Still," he murmured as if to himself, "a man who can burst an iron lock with his bare hands has scant need of weapons."

"You are wasting valuable time," I said impatiently. "I was sent here tonight to kill Sir Haldred Frenton--"

"By whom?" the question was shot at me.

"By the man who sometimes goes disguised as a leper."

He nodded, a gleam in his scintillant eyes.

"My suspicions were correct, then."

"Doubtless. Listen to me closely--do you desire the death or arrest of that man?"

Gordon laughed grimly.

"To one who wears the mark of the scorpion on his hand, my answer would be superfluous."

"Then follow my directions and your wish shall be granted."

His eyes narrowed suspiciously.

"So that was the meaning of this open entry and non-resistance," he said slowly. "Does the dope which dilates your eyeballs so warp your mind that you think to lead me into ambush?"

I pressed my hands against my temples. Time was racing and every moment was precious--how could I convince this man of my honesty?

"Listen; my name is Stephen Costigan of America. I was a frequenter of Yun Shatu's dive and a hashish addict--as you have guessed, but just now a slave of stronger dope. By virtue of this slavery, the man you know as a false leper, whom Yun Shatu and his friends call 'Master,' gained dominance over me and sent me here to murder Sir Haldred--why, God only knows. But I have gained a space of respite by coming into possession of some of this dope which I must have in order to live, and I fear and hate this Master. Listen to me and I swear, by all things holy and unholy, that before the sun rises the false leper shall be in your power!"

I could tell that Gordon was impressed in spite of himself.

"Speak fast!" he rapped.

Still I could sense his disbelief and a wave of futility swept over me.

"If you will not act with me," I said, "let me go and somehow I'll find a way to get to the Master and kill him. My time is short--my hours are numbered and my vengeance is yet to be realized."

"Let me hear your plan, and talk fast," Gordon answered.

"It is simple enough. I will return to the Masters lair and tell him I have accomplished that which he sent me to do. You must follow closely with your men and while I engage the Master in conversation, surround the house. Then, at the signal, break in and kill or seize him."

Gordon frowned. "Where is this house?"

"The warehouse back of Yun Shatu's has been converted into a veritable oriental palace."

"The warehouse!" he exclaimed. "How can that be? I had thought of that first, but I have carefully examined it from without. The windows are closely barred and spiders have built webs across them. The doors are nailed fast on the outside and the seals that mark the warehouse as deserted have never been broken or disturbed in any way."

"They tunneled up from beneath," I answered. "The Temple of Dreams is directly connected with the warehouse."

"I have traversed the alley between the two buildings," said Gordon, "and the doors of the warehouse opening into that alley are, as I have said, nailed shut from without just as the owners left them. There is apparently no rear exit of any kind from the Temple of Dreams."

"A tunnel connects the buildings, with one door in the rear room of Yun Shatu's and the other in the idol room of the warehouse."

"I have been in Yun Shatu's back room and found no such door."

"The table rests upon it. You noted the heavy table in the center of the room? Had you turned it around the secret door would have opened in the floor. Now this is my plan: I will go in through the Temple of Dreams and meet the Master in the idol room. You will have men secretly stationed in front of the warehouse and others upon the other street, in front of the Temple of Dreams. Yun Shatu's building, as you know, faces the waterfront, while the warehouse, fronting the opposite direction, faces a narrow street running parallel with the river. At the signal let the men in this street break open the front of the warehouse and rush in, while simultaneously those in front of Yun Shatu's make an invasion through the Temple of Dreams. Let these make for the rear room, shooting without mercy any who may seek to deter them, and there open the secret door as I have said. There being, to the best of my knowledge, no other exit from the Master's lair, he and his servants will necessarily seek to make their escape through the tunnel. Thus we will have them on both sides."

Gordon ruminated while I studied his face with breathless interest.

"This may be a snare," he muttered, "or an attempt to draw me away from Sir Haldred, but--"

I held my breath.

"I am a gambler by nature," he said slowly. "I am going to follow what you Americans call a hunch--but God help you if you are lying to me!"

I sprang erect.

"Thank God! Now aid me with this suit, for I must be wearing it when I return to the automobile waiting for me."

His eyes narrowed as I shook out the horrible masquerade and prepared to don it.

"This shows, as always, the touch of the master hand. You were doubtless instructed to leave marks of your hands, encased in those hideous gauntlets?"

"Yes, though I have no idea why."

"I think I have--the Master is famed for leaving no real clues to mark his crimes--a great ape escaped from a neighboring zoo earlier in the evening and it seems too obvious for mere chance, in the light of this disguise. The ape would have gotten the blame of Sir Haldred's death."

The thing was easily gotten into and the illusion of reality it created was so perfect as to draw a shudder from me as I viewed myself in a mirror.

"It is now two o'clock," said Gordon."Allowing for the time it will take you to get back to Limehouse and the time it will take me to get my men stationed, I promise you that at half-past four the house will be closely surrounded. Give me a start--wait here until I have left this house, so I will arrive at least as soon as you."

"Good!" I impulsively grasped his hand. "There will doubtless be a girl there who is in no way implicated with the Master's evil doings, but only a victim of circumstances such as I have been. Deal gently with her."

"It shall be done. What signal shall I look for?"

"I have no way of signaling for you and I doubt if any sound in the house could be heard on the street. Let your men make their raid on the stroke of five."

I turned to go.

"A man is waiting for you with a car, I take it? Is he likely to suspect anything?"

"I have a way of finding out, and if he does," I replied grimly, "I will return alone to the Temple of Dreams."

Chapter 11. Four Thirty-Four

"Doubting, dreaming dreams no mortal ever dared to dream before."

--Poe

The door closed softly behind me, the great dark house looming up more starkly than ever. Stooping, I crossed the wet lawn at a run, a grotesque and unholy figure, I doubt not, since any man had at a glance sworn me to be not a man but a giant ape. So craftily had the Master devised!

I clambered the wall, dropped to the earth beyond and made my way through the darkness and the drizzle to the group of trees which masked the automobile.

The Negro driver leaned out of the front seat. I was breathing hard and sought in various ways to simulate the actions of a man who has just murdered in cold blood and fled the scene of his crime.

"You heard nothing, no sound, no scream?" I hissed, gripping his arm.

"No noise except a slight crash when you first went in," he answered. "You did a good job--nobody passing along the road could have suspected anything."

"Have you remained in the car all the time?" I asked. And when he replied that he had, I seized his ankle and ran my hand over the soles of his shoe; it was perfectly dry, as was the cuff of his trouser leg. Satisfied, I climbed into the back seat. Had he taken a step on the earth, shoe and garment would have showed it by the telltale dampness.

I ordered him to refrain from starting the engine until I had removed the apeskin, and then we sped through the night and I fell victim to doubts and uncertainties. Why should Gordon put any trust in the word of a stranger and a former ally of the Master's? Would he not put my tale down as the ravings of a dope-crazed addict, or a lie to ensnare or befool him? Still, if he had not believed me, why had he let me go?

I could but trust. At any rate, what Gordon did or did not do would scarcely affect my fortunes ultimately, even though Zuleika had furnished me with that which would merely extend the number of my days. My thought centered on her, and more than my hope of vengeance on Kathulos was the hope that Gordon might be able to save her from the clutches of the fiend. At any rate, I thought grimly, if Gordon failed me, I still had my hands and if I might lay them upon the bony frame of the Skull-faced One--

Abruptly I found myself thinking of Yussef Ali and his strange words, the import of which just occurred to me, *"The Master has promised her to me in the days of the empire!"*

The days of the empire--what could that mean?

The automobile at last drew up in front of the building which hid the Temple of Silence--now dark and still. The ride had seemed interminable and as I dismounted I glanced at the timepiece on the dashboard of the car. My heart leaped--it was four thirty-four, and unless my eyes tricked me I saw a movement in the shadows across the street, out of the flare of the street lamp. At this time of night it could mean only one of two things--some menial of the Master watching for my return or else Gordon had kept his word. The Negro drove away and I opened the door, crossed the deserted bar and entered the opium room. The bunks and the floor were littered with the dreamers, for such places as these know nothing of day or night as normal people know, but all lay deep in sottish slumber.

The lamps glimmered through the smoke and a silence hung mist-like over all.

Chapter 12. The Stroke of Five

"He saw gigantic tracks of death,
And many a shape of doom."
--Chesterton

Two of the China-boys squatted among the smudge fires, staring at me unwinkingly as I threaded my way among the recumbent bodies and made my way to the rear door. For the first time I traversed the corridor alone and found time to wonder again as to the contents of the strange chests which lined the walls.

Four raps on the underside of the floor, and a moment later I stood in the idol room. I gasped in amazement--the fact that across a table from me sat Kathulos in all his horror was not the cause of my exclamation. Except for the table, the chair on which the Skull-faced One sat and the altar--now bare of incense--the room was perfectly bare! Drab, unlovely walls of the unused warehouse met my gaze instead of the costly tapestries I had become accustomed to. The palms, the idol, the lacquered screen--all were gone.

"Ah, Mr. Costigan, you wonder, no doubt."

The dead voice of the Master broke in on my thoughts. His serpent eyes glittered balefully. The long yellow fingers twined sinuously upon the table.

"You thought me to be a trusting fool, no doubt!" he rapped suddenly. "Did you think I would not have you followed? You fool, Yussef Ali was at your heels every moment!"

An instant I stood speechless, frozen by the crash of these words against my brain; then as their import sank home, I launched myself forward with a roar. At the same instant, before my clutching fingers could close on the mocking horror on the other side of the table, men rushed from every side. I whirled, and with the clarity of hate, from the swirl of savage faces I singled out Yussef Ali, and crashed my right fist against his temple with every ounce of my strength. Even as he dropped, Hassim struck me to my knees and a Chinaman flung a man-net over my shoulders. I heaved erect, bursting the stout cords as if they were strings, and then a blackjack in the hands of Ganra Singh stretched me stunned and bleeding on the floor.

Lean sinewy hands seized and bound me with cords that cut cruelly into my flesh. Emerging from the mists of semi-unconsciousness, I found myself lying on the altar with the masked Kathulos towering over me like a gaunt ivory tower. About in a semicircle stood Ganra Singh, Yar Khan, Yun Shatu and several others whom I knew as frequenters of the Temple of Dreams. Beyond them--and the sight cut me to the heart--I saw Zuleika crouching in a doorway, her face white and her hands pressed against her cheeks, in an attitude of abject terror.

"I did not fully trust you," said Kathulos sibilantly, "so I sent Yussef Ali to follow you. He reached the group of trees before you and following you into the estate heard your very interesting conversation with John Gordon--for he scaled the house-wall like a cat and clung to the window ledge! Your driver delayed purposely so as to give Yussef Ali plenty of time to get back--I have decided to change my abode anyway. My furnishings are already on their way to another house, and as soon as we have disposed of the traitor--you!--we shall depart also, leaving a little surprize for your friend Gordon when he arrives at five-thirty."

My heart gave a sudden leap of hope. Yussef Ali had misunderstood, and Kathulos lingered here in false security while the London detective force had already silently surrounded the house. Over my shoulder I saw Zuleika vanish from the door.

I eyed Kathulos, absolutely unaware of what he was saying. It was not long until five--if he dallied longer--then I froze as the Egyptian spoke a word and Li Kung, a gaunt, cadaverous Chinaman, stepped from the silent semicircle and drew from his sleeve a long thin dagger. My eyes sought the timepiece that still rested on the table and my heart sank. It was still ten minutes until five. My death did not matter so much, since it simply hastened the inevitable, but in my mind's eye I could see Kathulos and his murderers escaping while the police awaited the stroke of five.

The Skull-face halted in some harangue, and stood in a listening attitude. I believe his uncanny intuition warned him of danger. He spoke a quick staccato command to Li Kung and the Chinaman sprang forward, dagger lifted above my breast.

The air was suddenly supercharged with dynamic tension. The keen dagger-point hovered high above me--loud and clear sounded the skirl of a police whistle and on the heels of the sound there came a terrific crash from the front of the warehouse!

Kathulos leaped into frenzied activity. Hissing orders like a cat spitting, he sprang for the hidden door and the rest followed him. Things happened with the speed of a nightmare. Li Kung had followed the rest, but Kathulos flung a command over his shoulder and the Chinaman turned back and came rushing toward the altar where I lay, dagger high, desperation in his countenance.

A scream broke through the clamor and as I twisted desperately about to avoid the descending dagger, I caught a glimpse of Kathulos dragging Zuleika away. Then with a frenzied wrench I toppled from the altar just as Li Kung's dagger, grazing my breast, sank inches deep into the dark-stained surface and quivered there.

I had fallen on the side next to the wall and what was taking place in the room I could not see, but it seemed as if far away I could hear men screaming faintly and hideously. Then Li Kung wrenched his blade free and sprang, tigerishly, around the end of the altar. Simultaneously a revolver cracked from the doorway--the Chinaman spun clear around, the dagger flying from his hand--he slumped to the floor.

Gordon came running from the doorway where a few moments earlier Zuleika had stood, his pistol still smoking in his hand. At his heels were three rangy, clean-cut men in plain clothes. He cut my bonds and dragged me upright.

"Quick! Where have they gone?"

The room was empty of life save for myself, Gordon and his men, though two dead men lay on the floor.

I found the secret door and after a few seconds' search located the lever which opened it. Revolvers drawn, the men grouped about me and peered nervously into the dark stairway. Not a sound came up from the total darkness.

"This is uncanny!" muttered Gordon. "I suppose the Master and his servants went this way when they left the building--as they are certainly not here now!--and Leary and his men should have stopped them either in the tunnel itself or in the rear room of Yun Shatu's. At any rate, in either event they should have communicated with us by this time."

"Look out, sir!" one of the men exclaimed suddenly, and Gordon, with an ejaculation, struck out with his pistol barrel and crushed the life from a huge snake which had crawled silently up the steps from the blackness beneath.

"Let us see into this matter," said he, straightening.

But before he could step onto the first stair, I halted him; for, flesh crawling, I began dimly to understand something of what had happened--I began to understand the silence in the tunnel, the absence of the detectives, the screams I had heard some minutes previously while I lay on the altar. Examining the lever which opened the door, I found another smaller lever--I began to believe I knew what those mysterious chests in the tunnel contained.

"Gordon," I said hoarsely, "have you an electric torch?"

One of the men produced a large one.

"Direct the light into the tunnel, but as you value your life, do not put a foot upon the steps."

The beam of light struck through the shadows, lighting the tunnel, etching out boldly a scene that will haunt my brain all the rest of my life. On the floor of the tunnel, between the chests which now gaped open, lay two men who were members of London's finest secret service. Limbs twisted and faces horribly distorted they lay, and above and about them writhed, in long glittering scaly shimmerings, scores of hideous reptiles.

The clock struck five.

Chapter 13. The Blind Beggar Who Rode

*"He seemed a beggar such as lags
Looking for crusts and ale."*
--Chesterton

The cold gray dawn was stealing over the river as we stood in the deserted bar of the Temple of Dreams. Gordon was questioning the two men who had remained on guard outside the building while their unfortunate companion, went in to explore the tunnel.

"As soon as we heard the whistle, sir, Leary and Murken rushed the bar and broke into the opium room, while we waited here at the bar door according to orders. Right away several ragged dopers came tumbling out and we grabbed them. But no one else came out and we heard nothing from Leary and Murken; so we just waited until you came, sir."

"You saw nothing of a giant Negro, or of the Chinaman Yun Sha-tu?"

"No, sir. After a while the patrolmen arrived and we threw a cordon around the house, but no one was seen."

Gordon shrugged his shoulders; a few cursory questions had satisfied him that the captives were harmless addicts and he had them released.

"You are sure no one else came out?"

"Yes, sir--no, wait a moment. A wretched old blind beggar did come out, all rags and dirt and with a ragged girl leading him. We stopped him but didn't hold him--a wretch like that couldn't be harmful."

"No?" Gordon jerked out. "Which way did he go?"

"The girl led him down the street to the next block and then an automobile stopped and they got in and drove off, sir."

Gordon glared at him.

"The stupidity of the London detective has rightfully become an international jest," he said acidly. "No doubt it never occurred to you as being strange that a Limehouse beggar should ride about in his own automobile."

Then impatiently waving aside the man, who sought to speak further, he turned to me and I saw the lines of weariness beneath his eyes.

"Mr. Costigan, if you will come to my apartment we may be able to clear up some new things."

Chapter 14. The Black Empire

"Oh the new spears dipped in life-blood as the woman
shrieked in vain!

*Oh the days before the English! When will those days come
again?"*

--Mundy

Gordon struck a match and absently allowed it to flicker and go out
in his hand. His Turkish cigarette hung unlighted between his fingers.

"This is the most logical conclusion to be reached," he was saying.
"The weak link in our chain was lack of men. But curse it, one cannot
round up an army at two o'clock in the morning, even with the aid of
Scotland Yard. I went on to Limehouse, leaving orders for a number of
patrolmen to follow me as quickly as they could be got together, and
to throw a cordon about the house.

"They arrived too late to prevent the Master's servants slipping out
of the side doors and windows, no doubt, as they could easily do with
only Finnegan and Hansen on guard at the front of the building. However, they arrived in time to prevent the Master himself from slipping
out in that way--no doubt he lingered to effect his disguise and was
caught in that manner. He owes his escape to his craft and boldness
and to the carelessness of Finnegan and Hansen. The girl who accompanied him--"

"She was Zuleika, without doubt."

I answered listlessly, wondering anew what shackles bound her to
the Egyptian sorcerer.

"You owe your life to her," Gordon rapped, lighting another match.
"We were standing in the shadows in front of the warehouse, waiting
for the hour to strike, and of course ignorant as to what was going on
in the house, when a girl appeared at one of the barred windows and
begged us for God's sake to do something, that a man was being mur-

dered. So we broke in at once. However, she was not to be seen when we entered."

"She returned to the room, no doubt," I muttered, "and was forced to accompany the Master. God grant he knows nothing of her trickery."

"I do not know," said Gordon, dropping the charred match stem, "whether she guessed at our true identity or whether she just made the appeal in desperation.

"However, the main point is this: evidence points to the fact that, on hearing the whistle, Leary and Murken invaded Yun Shatu's from the front at the same instant my three men and I made our attack on the warehouse front. As it took us some seconds to batter down the door, it is logical to suppose that they found the secret door and entered the tunnel before we affected an entrance into the warehouse.

"The Master, knowing our plans beforehand, and being aware that an invasion would be made through the tunnel and having long ago made preparations for such an exigency--"

An involuntary shudder shook me.

"--the Master worked the lever that opened the chest--the screams you heard as you lay upon the altar were the death shrieks of Leary and Murken. Then, leaving the Chinaman behind to finish you, the Master and the rest descended into the tunnel--incredible as it seems-- and threading their way unharmed among the serpents, entered Yun Shatu's house and escaped therefrom as I have said."

"That seems impossible. Why should not the snakes turn on them?"

Gordon finally ignited his cigarette and puffed a few seconds before replying.

"The reptiles might still have been giving their full and hideous attention to the dying men, or else--I have on previous occasions been confronted with indisputable proof of the Master's dominance over beasts and reptiles of even the lowest or most dangerous orders. How he and his slaves passed unhurt among those scaly fiends must remain, at present, one of the many unsolved mysteries pertaining to that strange man."

I stirred restlessly in my chair. This brought up a point for the purpose of clearing up which I had come to Gordon's neat but bizarre apartments.

"You have not yet told me," I said abruptly, "who this man is and what is his mission."

"As to who he is, I can only say that he is known as you name him--the Master. I have never seen him unmasked, nor do I know his real name nor his nationality."

"I can enlighten you to an extent there," I broke in. "I have seen him unmasked and have heard the name his slaves call him."

Gordon's eyes blazed and he leaned forward.

"His name," I continued, "is Kathulos and he claims to be an Egyptian."

"Kathulos!" Gordon repeated. "You say he claims to be an Egyptian--have you any reason for doubting his claim of that nationality?"

"He may be of Egypt," I answered slowly, "but he is different, somehow, from any human I ever saw or hope to see. Great age might account for some of his peculiarities, but there are certain lineal differences that my anthropological studies tell me have been present since birth--features which would be abnormal to any other man but which are perfectly normal in Kathulos. That sounds paradoxical, I admit, but to appreciate fully the horrid inhumanness of the man, you would have to see him yourself."

Gordon sat at attention while I swiftly sketched the appearance of the Egyptian as I remembered him--and that appearance was indelibly etched on my brain forever.

As I finished he nodded.

"As I have said, I never saw Kathulos except when disguised as a beggar, a leper or some such thing--when he was fairly swathed in rags. Still, I too have been impressed with a strange difference about him--something that is not present in other men."

Gordon tapped his knee with his fingers--a habit of his when deeply engrossed by a problem of some sort.

"You have asked as to the mission of this man," he began slowly. "I will tell you all I know."

"My position with the British government is a unique and peculiar one. I hold what might be called a roving commission--an office created solely for the purpose of suiting my special needs. As a secret service official during the war, I convinced the powers of a need of such office and of my ability to fill it.

"Somewhat over seventeen months ago I was sent to South Africa to investigate the unrest which has been growing among the natives of the interior ever since the World War and which has of late assumed alarming proportions. There I first got on the track of this man Kathulos. I found, in roundabout ways, that Africa was a seething cauldron of rebellion from Morocco to Cape Town. The old, old vow had been made again--the Negroes and the Mohammedans, banded together, should drive the white men into the sea.

"This pact has been made before but always, hitherto, broken. Now, however, I sensed a giant intellect and a monstrous genius behind the veil, a genius powerful enough to accomplish this union and hold it together. Working entirely on hints and vague whispered clues, I followed the trail up through Central Africa and into Egypt. There, at last, I came upon definite evidence that such a man existed. The whispers hinted of a living dead man--a *skull-faced* man. I learned that this man was the high priest of the mysterious Scorpion society of northern Africa. He was spoken of variously as Skull-face, the Master, and the Scorpion.

"Following a trail of bribed officials and filched state secrets, I at last trailed him to Alexandria, where I had my first sight of him in a dive in the native quarter--disguised as a leper. I heard him distinctly addressed as 'Mighty Scorpion' by the natives, but he escaped me.

"All trace vanished then; the trail ran out entirely until rumors of strange happenings in London reached me and I came back to England to investigate an apparent leak in the war office.

"As I thought, the Scorpion had preceded me. This man, whose education and craft transcend anything I ever met with, is simply the leader and instigator of a world-wide movement such as the world has never seen before. He plots, in a word, the overthrow of the white races!

"His ultimate aim is a black empire, with himself as emperor of the world! And to that end he has banded together in one monstrous conspiracy the black, the brown and the yellow."

"I understand now what Yussef Ali meant when he said 'the days of the empire,'" I muttered.

"Exactly," Gordon rapped with suppressed excitement. "Kathulos' power is unlimited and unguessed. Like an octopus his tentacles stretch to the high places of civilization and the far corners of the world. And his main weapon is--dope! He has flooded Europe and no doubt America with opium and hashish, and in spite of all effort it has been impossible to discover the break in the barriers through which the hellish stuff is coming. With this he ensnares and enslaves men and women.

"You have told me of the aristocratic men and women you saw coming to Yun Shatu's dive. Without doubt they were dope addicts--for, as I said, the habit lurks in high places--holders of governmental positions, no doubt, coming to trade for the stuff they craved and giving in return state secrets, inside information and promise of protection for the Master's crimes.

"Oh, he does not work haphazardly! Before ever the black flood breaks, he will be prepared; if he has his way, the governments of the white races will be honeycombs of corruption--the strongest men of the white races will be dead. The white men's secrets of war will be his. When it comes, I look for a simultaneous uprising against white supremacy, of all the colored races--races who, in the last war, learned the white men's ways of battle, and who, led by such a man as Kathulos and armed with white men's finest weapons, will be almost invincible.

"A steady stream of rifles and ammunition has been pouring into East Africa and it was not until I discovered the source that it was stopped. I found that a staid and reliable Scotch firm was smuggling these arms among the natives and I found more: the manager of this firm was an opium slave. That was enough. I saw Kathulos' hand in the matter. The manager was arrested and committed suicide in his cell--that is only one of the many situations with which I am called upon to deal.

"Again, the case of Major Fairlan Morley. He, like myself, held a very flexible commission and had been sent to the Transvaal to work upon the same case. He sent to London a number of secret papers for safekeeping. They arrived some weeks ago and were put in a bank vault. The letter accompanying them gave explicit instructions that they were to be delivered to no one but the major himself, when he called for them in person, or in event of his death, to myself.

"As soon as I learned that he had sailed from Africa I sent trusted men to Bordeaux, where he intended to make his first landing in Europe. They did not succeed in saving the major's life, but they certified his death, for they found his body in a deserted ship whose hulk was stranded on the beach. Efforts were made to keep the affair a secret but somehow it leaked into the papers with the result--"

"I begin to understand why I was to impersonate the unfortunate major," I interrupted.

"Exactly. A false beard furnished you, and your black hair dyed blond, you would have presented yourself at the bank, received the papers from the banker, who knew Major Morley just intimately enough to be deceived by your appearance, and the papers would have then fallen into the hands of the Master.

"I can only guess at the contents of those papers, for events have been taking place too swiftly for me to call for and obtain them. But they must deal with subjects closely connected with the activities of Kathulos. How he learned of them and of the provisions of the letter accompanying them, I have no idea, but as I said, London is honeycombed with his spies.

"In my search for clues, I often frequented Limehouse disguised as you first saw me. I went often to the Temple of Dreams and even once managed to enter the back room, for I suspected some sort of rendezvous in the rear of the building. The absence of any exit baffled me and I had no time to search for secret doors before I was ejected by the giant black man Hassim, who had no suspicion of my true identity. I noticed that very often the leper entered or left Yun Shatu's, and finally it was borne on me that past a shadow of doubt this supposed leper was the Scorpion himself.

"That night you discovered me on the couch in the opium room, I had come there with no especial plan in mind. Seeing Kathulos leaving, I determined to rise and follow him, but you spoiled that."

He fingered his chin and laughed grimly.

"I was an amateur boxing champion in Oxford," said he, "but Tom Cribb himself could not have withstood that blow--or have dealt it."

"I regret it as I regret few things."

"No need to apologize. You saved my life immediately afterward--I was stunned, but not too much to know that that brown devil Yussef Ali was burning to cut out my heart."

"How did you come to be at Sir Haldred Frenton's estate? And how is it that you did not raid Yun Shatu's dive?"

"I did not have the place raided because I knew somehow Kathulos would be warned and our efforts would come to naught. I was at Sir Haldred's that night because I have contrived to spend at least part of each night with him since he returned from the Congo. I anticipated an attempt upon his life when I learned from his own lips that he was preparing, from the studies he made on this trip, a treatise on the secret native societies of West Africa. He hinted that the disclosures he intended to make therein might prove sensational, to say the least. Since it is to Kathulos' advantage to destroy such men as might be able to arouse the Western world to its danger, I knew that Sir Haldred was a marked man. Indeed, two distinct attempts were made upon his life on his journey to the coast from the African interior. So I put two trusted men on guard and they are at their post even now.

"Roaming about the darkened house, I heard the noise of your entry, and, warning my men, I stole down to intercept you. At the time of our conversation, Sir Haldred was sitting in his unlighted study, a

Scotland Yard man with drawn pistol on each side of him. Their vigilance no doubt accounts for Yussef Ali's failure to attempt what you were sent to do.

"Something in your manner convinced me in spite of yourself," he meditated. "I will admit I had some bad moments of doubt as I waited in the darkness that precedes dawn, outside the warehouse."

Gordon rose suddenly and going to a strong box which stood in a corner of the room, drew thence a thick envelope.

"Although Kathulos has checkmated me at almost every move," he said, "I have not been entirely idle. Noting the frequenters of Yun Shatu's, I have compiled a partial list of the Egyptian's right-hand men, and their records. What you have told me has enabled me to complete that list. As we know, his henchmen are scattered all over the world, and there are possibly hundreds of them here in London. However, this is a list of those I believe to be in his closest council, now with him in England. He told you himself that few even of his followers ever saw him unmasked."

We bent together over the list, which contained the following names: "Yun Shatu, Hongkong Chinese, suspected opium smuggler--keeper of Temple of Dreams--resident of Limehouse seven years. Hassim, ex-Senegalese Chief--wanted in French Congo for murder. Santiago, Negro--fled from Haiti under suspicion of voodoo worship atrocities. Yar Khan, Afridi, record unknown. Yussef Ali, Moor, slave-dealer in Morocco--suspected of being a German spy in the World War--an instigator of the Fellaheen Rebellion on the upper Nile. Ganra Singh, Lahore, India, Sikh--smuggler of arms into Afghanistan--took an active part in the Lahore and Delhi riots--suspected of murder on two occasions--a dangerous man. Stephen Costigan, American--resident in England since the war--hashish addict--man of remarkable strength. Li Kung, northern China, opium smuggler."

Lines were drawn significantly through three names--mine, Li Kung's and Yussef Ali's. Nothing was written next to mine, but following Li Kung's name was scrawled briefly in Gordon's rambling characters: "Shot by John Gordon during the raid on Yun Shatu's." And following the name of Yussef Ali: "Killed by Stephen Costigan during the Yun Shatu raid."

I laughed mirthlessly. Black empire or not, Yussef Ali would never hold Zuleika in his arms, for he had never risen from where I felled him.

"I know not," said Gordon somberly as he folded the list and replaced it in the envelope, "what power Kathulos has that draws together black men and yellow men to serve him--that unites world-old foes. Hindu, Moslem and pagan are among his followers. And back in the mists of the East where mysterious and gigantic forces are at work, this uniting is culminating on a monstrous scale."

He glanced at his watch.

"It is nearly ten. Make yourself at home here, Mr. Costigan, while I visit Scotland Yard and see if any clue has been found as to Kathulos' new quarters. I believe that the webs are closing on him, and with your aid I promise you we will have the gang located within a week at most."

Chapter 15. The Mark of the Tulwar

*"The fed wolf curls by his drowsy mate
In a tight-trod earth; but the lean wolves wait."*
--Mundy

I sat alone in John Gordon's apartments and laughed mirthlessly. In spite of the elixir's stimulus, the strain of the previous night, with its loss of sleep and its heartrending actions, was telling on me. My mind was a chaotic whirl wherein the faces of Gordon, Kathulos and Zuleika shifted with numbing swiftness. All the mass of information Gordon had given to me seemed jumbled and incoherent.

Through this state of being, one fact stood out boldly. I must find the latest hiding-place of the Egyptian and get Zuleika out of his hands--if indeed she still lived.

A week, Gordon had said--I laughed again--a week and I would be beyond aiding anyone. I had found the proper amount of elixir to use-- knew the minimum amount my system required--and knew that I could make the flask last me four days at most. Four days! Four days in which to comb the rat-holes of Limehouse and Chinatown--four days in which to ferret out, somewhere in the mazes of East End, the lair of Kathulos.

I burned with impatience to begin, but nature rebelled, and staggering to a couch, I fell upon it and was asleep instantly.

Then someone was shaking me.

"Wake up, Mr. Costigan!"

I sat up, blinking. Gordon stood over me, his face haggard.

"There's devil's work done, Costigan! The Scorpion has struck again!"

I sprang up, still half-asleep and only partly realizing what he was saying. He helped me into my coat, thrust my hat at me, and then his firm grip on my arm was propelling me out of his door and down the stairs. The street lights were blazing; I had slept an incredible time.

"A logical victim!" I was aware that my companion was saying. "He should have notified me the instant of his arrival!"

"I don't understand--" I began dazedly.

We were at the curb now and Gordon hailed a taxi, giving the address of a small and unassuming hotel in a staid and prim section of the city.

"The Baron Rokoff," he rapped as we whirled along at reckless speed, "a Russian free-lance, connected with the war office. He returned from Mongolia yesterday and apparently went into hiding. Undoubtedly he had learned something vital in regard to the slow waking of the East. He had not yet communicated with us, and I had no idea that he was in England until just now."

"And you learned--"

"The baron was found in his room, his dead body mutilated in a frightful manner!"

The respectable and conventional hotel which the doomed baron had chosen for his hiding-place was in a state of mild uproar, suppressed by the police. The management had attempted to keep the matter quiet, but somehow the guests had learned of the atrocity and many were leaving in haste--or preparing to, as the police were holding all for investigation.

The baron's room, which was on the top floor, was in a state to defy description. Not even in the Great War have I seen a more complete shambles. Nothing had been touched; all remained just as the chambermaid had found it a half-hour since. Tables and chairs lay shattered on the floor, and the furniture, floor and walls were spattered with blood. The baron, a tall, muscular man in life, lay in the middle of the room, a fearful spectacle. His skull had been cleft to the brows, a deep gash under his left armpit had shorn through his ribs, and his left arm hung by a shred of flesh. The cold bearded face was set in a look of indescribable horror.

"Some heavy, curved weapon must have been used," said Gordon, "something like a saber, wielded with terrific force. See where a chance blow sank inches deep into the windowsill. And again, the thick back of this heavy chair has been split like a shingle. A saber, surely."

"A tulwar," I muttered, somberly. "Do you not recognize the handiwork of the Central Asian butcher? Yar Khan has been here."

"The Afghan! He came across the roofs, of course, and descended to the window-ledge by means of a knotted rope made fast to something on the edge of the roof. About one-thirty the maid, passing through the corridor, heard a terrific commotion in the baron's room--smashing of chairs and a sudden short shriek which died abruptly into a ghastly gurgle and then ceased--to the sound of heavy blows, curiously muffled, such as a sword might make when driven deep into human flesh. Then all noises stopped suddenly.

"She called the manager and they tried the door and, finding it locked, and receiving no answer to their shouts, opened it with the desk key. Only the corpse was there, but the window was open. This is strangely unlike Kathulos' usual procedure. It lacks subtlety. Often his victims have appeared to have died from natural causes. I scarcely understand."

"I see little difference in the outcome," I answered. "There is nothing that can be done to apprehend the murderer as it is."

"True," Gordon scowled. "We know who did it but there is no proof--not even a fingerprint. Even if we knew where the Afghan is hiding and arrested him, we could prove nothing--there would be a score of men to swear alibis for him. The baron returned only yesterday. Kathulos probably did not know of his arrival until tonight. He knew that on the morrow Rokoff would make known his presence to me and impart what he learned in northern Asia. The Egyptian knew he must strike quickly, and lacking time to prepare a safer and more elaborate form of murder, he sent the Afridi with his tulwar. There is nothing we can do, at least not until we discover the Scorpion's hiding-place; what the baron had learned in Mongolia, we shall never know, but that it dealt with the plans and aspirations of Kathulos, we may be sure."

We went down the stairs again and out on the street, accompanied by one of the Scotland Yard men, Hansen. Gordon suggested that we walk back to his apartment and I greeted the opportunity to let the cool night air blow some of the cobwebs out of my mazed brain.

As we walked along the deserted streets, Gordon suddenly cursed savagely.

"This is a veritable labyrinth we are following, leading nowhere! Here, in the very heart of civilization's metropolis, the direct enemy of that civilization commits crimes of the most outrageous nature and goes free! We are children, wandering in the night, struggling with an unseen evil--dealing with an incarnate devil, of whose true identity we know nothing and whose true ambitions we can only guess.

"Never have we managed to arrest one of the Egyptian's direct henchmen, and the few dupes and tools of his we have apprehended have died mysteriously before they could tell us anything. Again I repeat: what strange power has Kathulos that dominates these men of different creeds and races? The men in London with him are, of course, mostly renegades, slaves of dope, but his tentacles stretch all over the East. Some dominance is his: the power that sent the Chinaman, Li Kung, back to kill you, in the face of certain death; that sent Yar Khan the Moslem over the roofs of London to do murder; that holds Zuleika the Circassian in unseen bonds of slavery.

"Of course we know," he continued after a brooding silence, "that the East has secret societies which are behind and above all considerations of creeds. There are cults in Africa and the Orient whose origin dates back to Ophir and the fall of Atlantis. This man must be a power in some or possibly all of these societies. Why, outside the Jews, I know of no oriental race which is so cordially despised by the other Eastern races, as the Egyptians! Yet here we have a man, an Egyptian by his own word, controlling the lives and destinies of orthodox Moslems, Hindus, Shintos and devil-worshippers. It's unnatural.

"Have you ever"--he turned to me abruptly--"heard the ocean mentioned in connection with Kathulos?"

"Never."

"There is a widespread superstition in northern Africa, based on a very ancient legend, that the great leader of the colored races would come out of the sea! And I once heard a Berber speak of the Scorpion as 'The Son of the Ocean.'"

"That is a term of respect among that tribe, is it not?"

"Yes; still I wonder sometimes."

Chapter 16. The Mummy Who Laughed

"Laughing as littered skulls that lie
After lost battles turn to the sky
An everlasting laugh."
--Chesterton

"A shop open this late," Gordon remarked suddenly.

A fog had descended on London and along the quiet street we were traversing the lights glimmered with the peculiar reddish haze characteristic of such atmospheric conditions. Our footfalls echoed drearily. Even in the heart of a great city there are always sections which seem overlooked and forgotten. Such a street was this. Not even a policeman was in sight.

The shop which had attracted Gordon's attention was just in front of us, on the same side of the street. There was no sign over the door, merely some sort of emblem, something like a dragon. Light flowed from the open doorway and the small show windows on each side. As it was neither a cafe nor the entrance to a hotel we found ourselves idly speculating over its reason for being open. Ordinarily, I suppose, neither of us would have given the matter a thought, but our nerves were so keyed up that we found ourselves instinctively suspicious of anything out of the ordinary. Then something occurred which was distinctly out of the ordinary.

A very tall, very thin man, considerably stooped, suddenly loomed up out of the fog in front of us, and beyond the shop. I had only a glance of him--an impression of incredible gauntness, of worn, wrinkled garments, a high silk hat drawn close over the brows, a face entirely hidden by a muffler; then he turned aside and entered the shop. A cold wind whispered down the street, twisting the fog into wispy ghosts, but the coldness that came upon me transcended the wind's.

"Gordon!" I exclaimed in a fierce, low voice; "my senses are no longer reliable or else Kathulos himself has just gone into that house!"

Gordon's eyes blazed. We were now close to the shop, and lengthening his strides into a run he hurled himself into the door, the detective and I close upon his heels.

A weird assortment of merchandise met our eyes. Antique weapons covered the walls, and the floor was piled high with curious things. Maori idols shouldered Chinese josses, and suits of medieval armor bulked darkly against stacks of rare oriental rugs and Latin-make shawls. The place was an antique shop. Of the figure who had aroused our interest we saw nothing.

An old man clad bizarrely in red fez, brocaded jacket and Turkish slippers came from the back of the shop; he was a Levantine of some sort.

"You wish something, sirs?"

"You keep open rather late," Gordon said abruptly, his eyes traveling swiftly over the shop for some secret hiding-place that might conceal the object of our search.

"Yes, sir. My customers number many eccentric professors and students who keep very irregular hours. Often the night boats unload special pieces for me and very often I have customers later than this. I remain open all night, sir."

"We are merely looking around," Gordon returned, and in an aside to Hansen: "Go to the back and stop anyone who tries to leave that way."

Hansen nodded and strolled casually to the rear of the shop. The back door was clearly visible to our view, through a vista of antique furniture and tarnished hangings strung up for exhibition. We had followed the Scorpion--if he it was--so closely that I did not believe he would have had time to traverse the full length of the shop and make his exit without our having seen him as we came in. For our eyes had been on the rear door ever since we had entered.

Gordon and I browsed around casually among the curios, handling and discussing some of them but I have no idea as to their nature. The Levantine had seated himself cross-legged on a Moorish mat close to the center of the shop and apparently took only a polite interest in our explorations.

After a time Gordon whispered to me: "There is no advantage in keeping up this pretense. We have looked everywhere the Scorpion might be hiding, in the ordinary manner. I will make known my identity and authority and we will search the entire building openly."

Even as he spoke a truck drew up outside the door and two burly Negroes entered. The Levantine seemed to have expected them, for he merely waved them toward the back of the shop and they responded with a grunt of understanding.

Gordon and I watched them closely as they made their way to a large mummy-case which stood upright against the wall not far from the back. They lowered this to a level position and then started for the door, carrying it carefully between them.

"Halt!" Gordon stepped forward, raising his hand authoritatively.

"I represent Scotland Yard," he said swiftly, "and have sanction for anything I choose to do. Set that mummy down; nothing leaves this shop until we have thoroughly searched it."

The Negroes obeyed without a word and my friend turned to the Levantine, who, apparently not perturbed or even interested, sat smoking a Turkish water-pipe.

"Who was that tall man who entered just before we did, and where did he go?"

"No one entered before you, sir. Or, if anyone did, I was at the back of the shop and did not see him. You are certainly at liberty to search my shop, sir."

And search it we did, with the combined craft of a secret service expert and a denizen of the underworld--while Hansen stood stolidly at his post, the two Negroes standing over the carved mummy-case watched us impassively and the Levantine sitting like a sphinx on his mat, puffing a fog of smoke into the air. The whole thing had a distinct effect of unreality.

At last, baffled, we returned to the mummy-case, which was certainly long enough to conceal even a man of Kathulos' height. The thing did not appear to be sealed as is the usual custom, and Gordon opened it without difficulty. A formless shape, swathed in moldering wrappings, met our eyes. Gordon parted some of the wrappings and revealed an inch or so of withered, brownish, leathery arm. He shuddered involuntarily as he touched it, as a man will do at the touch of a reptile or some inhumanly cold thing. Taking a small metal idol from a stand nearby, he rapped on the shrunken breast and the arm. Each gave out a solid thumping, like some sort of wood.

Gordon shrugged his shoulders. "Dead for two thousand years anyway and I don't suppose I should risk destroying a valuable mummy simply to prove what we know to be true."

He closed the case again.

"The mummy may have crumbled some, even from this much exposure, but perhaps it did not."

This last was addressed to the Levantine who replied merely by a courteous gesture of his hand, and the Negroes once more lifted the case and carried it to the truck, where they loaded it on, and a moment later mummy, truck and Negroes had vanished in the fog.

Gordon still nosed about the shop, but I stood stock-still in the center of the floor. To my chaotic and dope-ridden brain I attribute it, but the sensation had been mine, that through the wrappings of the mummy's face, great eyes had burned into mine, eyes like pools of yellow fire, that seared my soul and froze me where I stood. And as the case had been carried through the door, I knew that the lifeless thing in it, dead, God only knows how many centuries, was laughing, hideously and silently.

Chapter 17. The Dead Man from the Sea

"The blind gods roar and rave and dream
Of all cities under the sea."
--Chesterton

Gordon puffed savagely at his Turkish cigarette, staring abstractedly and unseeingly at Hansen, who sat opposite him.

"I suppose we must chalk up another failure against ourselves. That Levantine, Kamonos, is evidently a creature of the Egyptian's and the walls and floors of his shop are probably honeycombed with secrét panels and doors which would baffle a magician."

Hansen made some answer but I said nothing. Since our return to Gordon's apartment, I had been conscious of a feeling of intense languor and sluggishness which not even my condition could account for. I knew that my system was full of the elixir--but my mind seemed strangely slow and hard of comprehension in direct contrast with the average state of my mentality when stimulated by the hellish dope.

This condition was slowly leaving me, like mist floating from the surface of a lake, and I felt as if I were waking gradually from a long and unnaturally sound sleep.

Gordon was saying: "I would give a good deal to know if Kamonos is really one of Kathulos' slaves or if the Scorpion managed to make his escape through some natural exit as we entered."

"Kamonos is his servant, true enough," I found myself saying slowly, as if searching for the proper words. "As we left, I saw his gaze light upon the scorpion which is traced on my hand. His eyes narrowed, and as we were leaving he contrived to brush close against me--and to whisper in a quick low voice: 'Soho, 48.'"

Gordon came erect like a loosened steel bow.

"Indeed!" he rapped. "Why did you not tell me at the time?"

"I don't know."

My friend eyed me sharply.

"I noticed you seemed like a man intoxicated all the way from the shop," said he. "I attributed it to some aftermath of hashish. But no. Kathulos is undoubtedly a masterful disciple of Mesmer--his power over venomous reptiles shows that, and I am beginning to believe it is the real source of his power over humans.

"Somehow, the Master caught you off your guard in that shop and partly asserted his dominance over your mind. From what hidden nook he sent his thought waves to shatter your brain, I do not know, but Kathulos was somewhere in that shop, I am sure."

"He was. He was in the mummy-case."

"The mummy-case!" Gordon exclaimed rather impatiently. "That is impossible! The mummy quite filled it and not even such a thin being as the Master could have found room there."

I shrugged my shoulders, unable to argue the point but somehow sure of the truth of my statement.

"Kamonos," Gordon continued, "doubtless is not a member of the inner circle and does not know of your change of allegiance. Seeing the mark of the scorpion, he undoubtedly supposed you to be a spy of the Master's. The whole thing may be a plot to ensnare us, but I feel that the man was sincere--Soho 48 can be nothing less than the Scorpion's new rendezvous."

I too felt that Gordon was right, though a suspicion lurked in my mind.

"I secured the papers of Major Morley yesterday," be continued, "and while you slept, I went over them. Mostly they but corroborated what I already knew--touched on the unrest of the natives and repeated the theory that one vast genius was behind all. But there was one matter which interested me greatly and which I think will interest you also."

From his strong box he took a manuscript written in the close, neat characters of the unfortunate major, and in a monotonous droning voice which betrayed little of his intense excitement he read the following nightmarish narrative:

"This matter I consider worth jotting down--as to whether it has any bearing on the case at hand, further developments will show. At Alexandria, where I spent some weeks seeking further clues as to the identity of the man known as the Scorpion, I made the acquaintance, through my friend Ahmed Shah, of the noted Egyptologist Professor Ezra Schuyler of New York. He verified the statement made by various laymen, concerning the legend of the 'ocean-man.' This myth, handed down from generation to generation, stretches back into the very mists of antiquity and is, briefly, that someday a man shall come up out of the sea and shall lead the people of Egypt to victory over all others. This legend has spread over the continent so that now all black races consider that it deals with the coming of a universal emperor. Professor Schuyler gave it as his opinion that the myth was somehow connected with the lost Atlantis, which, he maintains, was located between the African and South American continents and to whose inhabitants the ancestors of the Egyptians were tributary. The reasons for his connection are too lengthy and vague to note here, but following the line of his theory he told me a strange and fantastic tale. He said that a close friend of his, Von Lorfmon of Germany, a sort of free-lance scientist, now dead, was sailing off the coast of Senegal some years ago, for the purpose of investigating and classifying the rare specimens of sea life found there. He was using for his purpose a small trading-vessel, manned by a crew of Moors, Greeks and Negroes.

"Some days out of sight of land, something floating was sighted, and this object, being grappled and brought aboard, proved to be a mummy-case of a most curious kind. Professor Schuyler explained to me the features whereby it differed from the ordinary Egyptian style, but from his rather technical account I merely got the impression that it was a strangely shaped affair carved with characters neither cuneiform nor hieroglyphic. The case was heavily lacquered, being watertight and airtight, and Von Lorfmon had considerable difficulty in opening it. However, he managed to do so without damaging the case, and a most unusual mummy was revealed. Schuyler said that he never saw either the mummy or the case, but that from descriptions given him by the Greek skipper who was present at the opening of the case, the mummy differed as much from the ordinary man as the case differed from the conventional type.

"Examination proved that the subject had not undergone the usual procedure of mummification. All parts were intact just as in life, but the whole form was shrunk and hardened to a wood-like consistency. Cloth wrappings swathed the thing and they crumbled to dust and vanished the instant air was let in upon them.

"Von Lorfmon was impressed by the effect upon the crew. The Greeks showed no interest beyond that which would ordinarily be shown by any man, but the Moors, and even more the Negroes, seemed to be rendered temporarily insane! As the case was hoisted on board, they all fell prostrate on the deck and raised a sort of worshipful chant, and it was necessary to use force in order to exclude them from the cabin wherein the mummy was exposed. A number of fights broke out between them and the Greek element of the crew, and the skipper and Von Lorfmon thought best to put back to the nearest port in all haste. The skipper attributed it to the natural aversion of seamen toward having a corpse on board, but Von Lorfmon seemed to sense a deeper meaning.

"They made port in Lagos, and that very night Von Lorfmon was murdered in his stateroom and the mummy and its case vanished. All the Moor and Negro sailors deserted ship the same night. Schuyler said--and here the matter took on a most sinister and mysterious aspect--that immediately afterward this widespread unrest among the natives began to smolder and take tangible form; he connected it in some manner with the old legend.

"An aura of mystery, also, hung over Von Lorfmon's death. He had taken the mummy into his stateroom, and anticipating an attack from the fanatical crew, had carefully barred and bolted door and portholes. The skipper, a reliable man, swore that it was virtually impossible to affect an entrance from without. And what signs were present pointed to the fact that the locks had been worked from within. The scientist was killed by a dagger which formed part of his collection and which was left in his breast.

"As I have said, immediately afterward the African cauldron began to seethe. Schuyler said that in his opinion the natives considered the ancient prophecy fulfilled. The mummy was the man from the sea.

"Schuyler gave as his opinion that the thing was the work of Atlanteans and that the man in the mummy-case was a native of lost Atlantis. How the case came to float up through the fathoms of water which cover the forgotten land, he does not venture to offer a theory. He is sure that somewhere in the ghost-ridden mazes of the African jungles the mummy has been enthroned as a god, and, inspired by the dead thing, the black warriors are gathering for a wholesale massacre. He believes, also, that some crafty Moslem is the direct moving power of the threatened rebellion."

Gordon ceased and looked up at me.

"Mummies seem to weave a weird dance through the warp of the tale," he said. "The German scientist took several pictures of the mummy with his camera, and it was after seeing these--which strangely enough were not stolen along with the thing--that Major Morley began to think himself on the brink of some monstrous discovery. His diary reflects his state of mind and becomes incoherent--his condition seems to have bordered on insanity. What did he learn to unbalance him so? Do you suppose that the mesmeric spells of Kathulos were used against him?"

"These pictures--" I began.

"They fell into Schuyler's hands and he gave one to Morley. I found it among the manuscripts."

He handed the thing to me, watching me narrowly. I stared, then rose unsteadily and poured myself a tumbler of wine.

"'Not a dead idol in a voodoo hut," I said shakily, "but a monster animated by fearsome life, roaming the world for victims. Morley had seen the Master--that is why his brain crumbled. Gordon, as I hope to live again, *that face is the face of Kathulos* !"

Gordon stared wordlessly at me.

"The Master hand, Gordon," I laughed. A certain grim enjoyment penetrated the mists of my horror, at the sight of the steel-nerved Englishman struck speechless, doubtless for the first time in his life.

He moistened his lips and said in a scarcely recognizable voice, "Then, in God's name, Costigan, nothing is stable or certain, and mankind hovers at the brink of untold abysses of nameless horror. If that dead monster found by Von Lorfmon be in truth the Scorpion, brought to life in some hideous fashion, what can mortal effort do against him?"

"The mummy at Kamonos'--" I began.

"Aye, the man whose flesh, hardened by a thousand years of non-existence--that must have been Kathulos himself! He would have just had time to strip, wrap himself in the linens and step into the case before we entered. You remember that the case, leaning upright against the wall, stood partly concealed by a large Burmese idol, which obstructed our view and doubtless gave him time to accomplish his purpose. My God, Costigan, with what horror of the prehistoric world are we dealing?"

"I have heard of Hindu fakirs who could induce a condition closely resembling death," I began. "Is it not possible that Kathulos, a shrewd and crafty Oriental, could have placed himself in this state and his followers have placed the case in the ocean where it was sure to be found? And might not he have been in this shape tonight at Kamonos'?"

Gordon shook his head.

"No, I have seen these fakirs. None of them ever feigned death to the extent of becoming shriveled and hard--in a word, dried up. Morley, narrating in another place the description of the mummy-case as jotted down by Von Lorfmon and passed on to Schuyler, mentions the fact that large portions of seaweed adhered to it--seaweed of a kind found only at great depths, on the bottom of the ocean. The wood, too, was of a kind which Von Lorfmon failed to recognize or to classify, in spite of the fact that he was one of the greatest living authorities on flora. And his notes again and again emphasize the enormous age of the thing. He admitted that there was no way of telling how old the mummy was, but his hints intimate that he believed it to be, not thousands of years old, but millions of years!

"No. We must face the facts. Since you are positive that the picture of the mummy is the picture of Kathulos--and there is little room for fraud--one of two things is practically certain: the Scorpion was never dead but ages ago was placed in that mummy-case and his life preserved in some manner, or else--he was dead and has been brought to life! Either of these theories, viewed in the cold light of reason, is absolutely untenable. Are we all insane?"

"Had you ever walked the road to hashish land," I said somberly, "you could believe anything to be true. Had you ever gazed into the terrible reptilian eyes of Kathulos the sorcerer, you would not doubt that he was both dead and alive."

Gordon gazed out the window, his fine face haggard in the gray light which had begun to steal through them.

"At any rate," said he, "there are two places which I intend exploring thoroughly before the sun rises again--Kamonos' antique shop and Soho 48."

Chapter 18. The Grip of the Scorpion

*"While from a proud tower in the town
Death looks gigantically down."*
--Poe

Hansen snored on the bed as I paced the room. Another day had passed over London and again the street lamps glimmered through the fog. Their lights affected me strangely. They seemed to beat, solid waves of energy, against my brain. They twisted the fog into strange sinister shapes. Footlights of the stage that is the streets of London, how many grisly scenes had they lighted? I pressed my hands hard against my throbbing temples, striving to bring my thoughts back from the chaotic labyrinth where they wandered.

Gordon I had not seen since dawn. Following the clue of "Soho 48" he had gone forth to arrange a raid upon the place and he thought it best that I should remain under cover. He anticipated an attempt upon my life, and again he feared that if I went searching among the dives I formerly frequented it would arouse suspicion.

Hansen snored on. I seated myself and began to study the Turkish shoes which clothed my feet. Zuleika had worn Turkish slippers--how she floated through my waking dreams, gilding prosaic things with her witchery! Her face smiled at me from the fog; her eyes shone from the flickering lamps; her phantom footfalls re-echoed through the misty chambers of my skull.

They beat an endless tattoo, luring and haunting till it seemed that these echoes found echoes in the hallway outside the room where I stood, soft and stealthy. A sudden rap at the door and I started.

Hansen slept on as I crossed the room and flung the door swiftly open. A swirling wisp of fog had invaded the corridor, and through it, like a silver veil, I saw her--Zuleika stood before me with her shimmering hair and her red lips parted and her great dark eyes.

Like a speechless fool I stood and she glanced quickly down the hallway and then stepped inside and closed the door.

"Gordon!" she whispered in a thrilling undertone. "Your friend! The Scorpion has him!"

Hansen had awakened and now sat gaping stupidly at the strange scene which met his eyes.

Zuleika did not heed him.

"And oh, Steephen!" she cried, and tears shone in her eyes, "I have tried so hard to secure some more elixir but I could not."

"Never mind that," I finally found my speech. "'Tell me about Gordon."

"He went back to Kamonos' alone, and Hassim and Ganra Singh took him captive and brought him to the Master's house. Tonight assemble a great host of the people of the Scorpion for the sacrifice."

"Sacrifice!" A grisly thrill of horror coursed down my spine. Was there no limit to the ghastliness of this business?

"Quick, Zuleika, where is this house of the Master's?"

"Soho, 48. You must summon the police and send many men to surround it, but you must not go yourself--"

Hansen sprang up quivering for action, but I turned to him. My brain was clear now, or seemed to be, and racing unnaturally.

"Wait!" I turned back to Zuleika. "When is this sacrifice to take place?"

"At the rising of the moon."

"That is only a few hours before dawn. Time to save him, but if we raid the house they'll kill him before we can reach them. And God only knows how many diabolical things guard all approaches."

"I do not know," Zuleika whimpered. "I must go now, or the Master will kill me."

Something gave way in my brain at that; something like a flood of wild and terrible exultation swept over me.

"The Master will kill no one!" I shouted, flinging my arms on high. "Before ever the east turns red for dawn, the Master dies! By all things holy and unholy I swear it!"

Hansen stared wildly at me and Zuleika shrank back as I turned on her. To my dope-inspired brain had come a sudden burst of light, true and unerring. I knew Kathulos was a mesmerist--that he understood fully the secret of dominating another's mind and soul. And I knew that at last I had hit upon the reason of his power over the girl. Mesmerism! As a snake fascinates and draws to him a bird, so the Master held Zuleika to him with unseen shackles. So absolute was his rule over her that it held even when she was out of his sight, working over great distances.

There was but one thing which would break that hold: the magnetic power of some other person whose control was stronger with her than Kathulos'. I laid my hands on her slim little shoulders and made her face me.

"Zuleika," I said commandingly, "here you are safe; you shall not return to Kathulos. There is no need of it. Now you are free."

But I knew I had failed before I ever started. Her eyes held a look of amazed, unreasoning fear and she twisted timidly in my grasp.

"Steephen, please let me go!" she begged. "I must--I must!"

I drew her over to the bed and asked Hansen for his handcuffs. He handed them to me, wonderingly, and I fastened one cuff to the bed-post and the other to her slim wrist. The girl whimpered but made no resistance, her limpid eyes seeking mine in mute appeal.

It cut me to the quick to enforce my will upon her in this apparently brutal manner but I steeled myself.

"Zuleika," I said tenderly, "you are now my prisoner. The Scorpion cannot blame you for not returning to him when you are unable to do so--and before dawn you shall be free of his rule entirely."

I turned to Hansen and spoke in a tone which admitted of no argument.

"Remain here, just without the door, until I return. On no account allow any strangers to enter--that is, anyone whom you do not personally know. And I charge you, on your honor as a man, do not release this girl, no matter what she may say. If neither I nor Gordon have returned by ten o'clock tomorrow, take her to this address--that family once was friends of mine and will take care of a homeless girl. I am going to Scotland Yard."

"Steephen," Zuleika wailed, "you are going to the Master's lair! You will be killed. Send the police, do not go!"

I bent, drew her into my arms, felt her lips against mine, then tore myself away.

The fog plucked at me with ghostly fingers, cold as the hands of dead men, as I raced down the street. I had no plan, but one was forming in my mind, beginning to seethe in the stimulated cauldron that was my brain. I halted at the sight of a policeman pacing his beat, and beckoning him to me, scribbled a terse note on a piece of paper torn from a notebook and handed it to him.

"Get this to Scotland Yard; it's a matter of life and death and it has to do with the business of John Gordon."

At that name, a gloved hand came up in swift assent, but his assurance of haste died out behind me as I renewed my flight. The note stated briefly that Gordon was a prisoner at Soho 48 and advised an immediate raid in force--advised, nay, in Gordon's name, commanded it.

My reason for my actions was simple; I knew that the first noise of the raid sealed John Gordon's doom. Somehow I first must reach him and protect or free him before the police arrived.

The time seemed endless, but at last the grim gaunt outlines of the house that was Soho 48 rose up before me, a giant ghost in the fog. The hour grew late; few people dared the mists and the dampness as I came to a halt in the street before this forbidding building. No lights showed from the windows, either upstairs or down. It seemed deserted. But the lair of the scorpion often seems deserted until the silent death strikes suddenly.

Here I halted and a wild thought struck me. One way or another, the drama would be over by dawn. Tonight was the climax of my career, the ultimate top of life. Tonight I was the strongest link in the strange chain of events. Tomorrow it would not matter whether I lived or died. I drew the flask of elixir from my pocket and gazed at it. Enough for two more days if properly eked out. Two more days of life! Or--I needed stimulation as I never needed it before; the task in front of me was one no mere human could hope to accomplish. If I drank the entire remainder of the elixir, I had no idea as to the duration of its effect, but it would last the night through. And my legs were shaky; my mind had curious periods of utter vacuity; weakness of brain and body assailed me. I raised the flask and with one draft drained it.

For an instant I thought it was death. Never had I taken such an amount.

Sky and world reeled and I felt as if I would fly into a million vibrating fragments, like the bursting of a globe of brittle steel. Like fire, like hell-fire the elixir raced along my veins and I was a giant! A monster! A superman!

Turning, I strode to the menacing, shadowy doorway. I had no plan; I felt the need of none. As a drunken man walks blithely into danger, I strode to the lair of the Scorpion, magnificently aware of my superiority, imperially confident of my stimulation and sure as the unchanging stars that the way would open before me.

Oh, there never was a superman like that who knocked commandingly on the door of Soho 48 that night in the rain and the fog!

I knocked four times, the old signal that we slaves had used to be admitted into the idol room at Yun Shatu's. An aperture opened in the center of the door and slanted eyes looked warily out. They slightly widened as the owner recognized me, then narrowed wickedly.

"You fool!" I said angrily. "Don't you see the mark?"

I held my hand to the aperture.

"Don't you recognize me? Let me in, curse you."

I think the very boldness of the trick made for its success. Surely by now all the Scorpion's slaves knew of Stephen Costigan's rebellion, knew that he was marked for death. And the very fact that I came there, inviting doom, confused the doorman.

The door opened and I entered. The man who had admitted me was a tall, lank Chinaman I had known as a servant at Kathulos. He closed the door behind me and I saw we stood in a sort of vestibule, lighted by a dim lamp whose glow could not be seen from the street for the reason that the windows were heavily curtained. The Chinaman glowered at me undecided. I looked at him, tensed. Then suspicion flared in his eyes and his hand flew to his sleeve. But at the instant I was on him and his lean neck broke like a rotten bough between my hands.

I eased his corpse to the thickly carpeted floor and listened. No sound broke the silence. Stepping as stealthily as a wolf, fingers spread like talons, I stole into the next room. This was furnished in oriental style, with couches and rugs and gold-worked drapery, but was empty of human life. I crossed it and went into the next one. Light flowed softly from the censers which were swung from the ceiling, and the Eastern rugs deadened the sound of my footfalls; I seemed to be moving through a castle of enchantment.

Every moment I expected a rush of silent assassins from the doorways or from behind the curtains or screen with their writhing dragons. Utter silence reigned. Room after room I explored and at last halted at the foot of the stairs. The inevitable censer shed an uncertain light, but most of the stairs were veiled in shadows. What horrors awaited me above?

But fear and the elixir are strangers and I mounted that stair of lurking terror as boldly as I had entered that house of terror. The upper rooms I found to be much like those below and with them they had this fact in common: they were empty of human life. I sought an attic but there seemed no door letting into one. Returning to the first floor, I made a search for an entrance into the basement, but again my efforts were fruitless. The amazing truth was borne in upon me: except for myself and that dead man who lay sprawled so grotesquely in the outer vestibule, there were no men in that house, dead or living.

I could not understand it. Had the house been bare of furniture I should have reached the natural conclusion that Kathulos had fled--but no signs of flight met my eye. This was unnatural, uncanny. I stood in the great shadowy library and pondered. No, I had made no mistake in the house. Even if the broken corpse in the vestibule were not there to furnish mute testimony, everything in the room pointed toward the presence of the Master. There were the artificial palms, the lacquered screens, the tapestries, even the idol, though now no incense smoke rose before it. About the walls were ranged long shelves of books, bound in strange and costly fashion--books in every language in the world, I found from a swift examination, and on every subject--outre and bizarre, most of them.

Remembering the secret passage in the Temple of Dreams, I investigated the heavy mahogany table which stood in the center of the room. Bur nothing resulted. A sudden blaze of fury surged up in me, primitive and unreasoning. I snatched a statuette from the table and dashed it against the shelf-covered wall. The noise of its breaking would surely bring the gang from their hiding-place. But the result was much more startling than that!

The statuette struck the edge of a shelf and instantly the whole section of shelves with their load of books swung silently outward, revealing a narrow doorway! As in the other secret door, a row of steps led downward. At another time I would have shuddered at the thought of descending, with the horrors of the other tunnel fresh in my mind, but inflamed as I was by the elixir, I strode forward without an instant's hesitancy.

Since there was no one in the house, they must be somewhere in the tunnel or in whatever lair to which the tunnel led. I stepped through the doorway, leaving the door open; the police might find it that way and follow me, though somehow I felt as if mine would be a lone hand from start to grim finish.

I went down a considerable distance and then the stair debouched into a level corridor some twenty feet wide--a remarkable thing. In spite of the width, the ceiling was rather low and from it hung small, curiously shaped lamps which flung a dim light. I stalked hurriedly along the corridor like old Death seeking victims, and as I went I noted the work of the thing. The floor was of great broad flags and the walls seemed to be of huge blocks of evenly set stone. This passage was clearly no work of modern days; the slaves of Kathulos never tunneled there. Some secret way of medieval times, I thought--and after all, who knows what catacombs lie below London, whose secrets are greater and darker than those of Babylon and Rome?

On and on I went, and now I knew that I must be far below the earth. The air was dank and heavy, and cold moisture dripped from the stones of walls and ceiling. From time to time I saw smaller passages leading away in the darkness but I determined to keep to the larger main one.

A ferocious impatience gripped me. I seemed to have been walking for hours and still only dank damp walls and bare flags and guttering lamps met my eyes. I kept a close watch for sinister-appearing chests or the like--saw no such things.

Then as I was about to burst into savage curses, another stair loomed up in the shadows in front of me.

Chapter 19. Dark Fury

"The ringed wolf glared the circle round
Through baleful, blue-lit eye,
Not unforgetful of his debt.
Quoth he, 'I'll do some damage yet
Or ere my turn to die!'"
--Mundy

Like a lean wolf I glided up the stairs. Some twenty feet up there was a sort of landing from which other corridors diverged, much like the lower one by which I had come. The thought came to me that the earth below London must be honeycombed with such secret passages, one above the other.

Some feet above this landing the steps halted at a door, and here I hesitated, uncertain as to whether I should chance knocking or not. Even as I meditated, the door began to open. I shrank back against the wall, flattening myself out as much as possible. The door swung wide and a Moor came through. Only a glimpse I had of the room beyond, out of the corner of my eye, but my unnaturally alert senses registered the fact that the room was empty.

And on the instant, before be could turn, I smote the Moor a single deathly blow behind the angle of the jawbone and be toppled headlong down the stairs, to lie in a crumpled heap on the landing, his limbs tossed grotesquely about.

My left hand caught the door as it started to slam shut and in an instant I was through and standing in the room beyond. As I had thought, there was no occupant of this room. I crossed it swiftly and entered the next. These rooms were furnished in a manner before which the furnishings of the Soho house paled into insignificance. Barbaric, terrible, unholy--these words alone convey some slight idea of the ghastly sights which met my eyes. Skulls, bones and complete skeletons formed much of the decorations, if such they were. Mummies leered from their cases and mounted reptiles ranged the walls. Between these sinister relics hung African shields of hide and bamboo, crossed with assegais and war daggers. Here and there reared obscene idols, black and horrible.

And in between and scattered about among these evidences of savagery and barbarism were vases, screens, rugs and hangings of the highest oriental workmanship; a strange and incongruous effect.

I had passed through two of these rooms without seeing a human being, when I came to stairs leading upward. Up these I went, several flights, until I came to a door in a ceiling. I wondered if I was still under the earth. Surely the first stairs had let into a house of some sort. I raised the door cautiously. Starlight met my eyes and I drew myself warily up and out. There I halted. A broad flat roof stretched away on all sides and beyond its rim on all sides glimmered the lights of London. Just what building I was on, I had no idea, but that it was a tall one I could tell, for I seemed to be above most of the lights I saw. Then I saw that I was not alone.

Over against the shadows of the ledge that ran around the roof's edge, a great menacing form bulked in starlight. A pair of eyes glinted at me with a light not wholly sane; the starlight glanced silver from a curving length of steel. Yar Khan the Afghan killer fronted me in the silent shadows.

A fierce wild exultation surged over me. Now I could begin to pay the debt I owed Kathulos and all his hellish band! The dope fired my veins and sent waves of inhuman power and dark fury through me. A spring and I was on my feet in a silent, deathly rush.

Yar Khan was a giant, taller and bulkier than I. He held a tulwar, and from the instant I saw him I knew that he was full of the dope to the use of which he was addicted--heroin.

As I came in he swung his heavy weapon high in the air, but ere he could strike I seized his sword wrist in an iron grip and with my free hand drove smashing blows into his midriff.

Of that hideous battle, fought in silence above the sleeping city with only the stars to see, I remember little. I remember tumbling back and forth, locked in a death embrace. I remember the stiff beard rasping my flesh as his dope-fired eyes gazed wildly into mine. I remember the taste of hot blood in my mouth, the tang of fearful exultation in my soul, the onrushing and upsurging of inhuman strength and fury.

God, what a sight for a human eye, had anyone looked upon that grim roof where two human leopards, dope maniacs, tore each other to pieces!

I remember his arm breaking like rotten wood in my grip and the tulwar falling from his useless hand. Handicapped by a broken arm, the end was inevitable, and with one wild uproaring flood of might, I rushed him to the edge of the roof and bent him backward far out over the ledge. An instant we struggled there; then I tore loose his hold and hurled him over, and one single shriek came up as he hurtled into the darkness below.

I stood upright, arms hurled up toward the stars, a terrible statue of primordial triumph. And down my breast trickled streams of blood from the long wounds left by the Afghan's frantic nails, on neck and face.

Then I turned with the craft of the maniac. Had no one heard the sound of that battle? My eyes were on the door through which I had come, but a noise made me turn, and for the first time I noticed a small affair like a tower jutting up from the roof. There was no window there, but there was a door, and even as I looked that door opened and a huge black form framed itself in the light that streamed from within. Hassim!

He stepped out on the roof and closed the door, his shoulders hunched and neck outthrust as he glanced this way and that. I struck him senseless to the roof with one hate-driven smash. I crouched over him, waiting some sign of returning consciousness; then away in the sky close to the horizon, I saw a faint red tint. The rising of the moon!

Where in God's name was Gordon? Even as I stood undecided, a strange noise reached me. It was curiously like the droning of many bees.

Striding in the direction from which it seemed to come, I crossed the roof and leaned over the ledge. A sight nightmarish and incredible met my eyes.

Some twenty feet below the level of the roof on which I stood, there was another roof, of the same size and clearly a part of the same building. On one side it was bounded by the wall; on the other three sides a parapet several feet high took the place of a ledge.

A great throng of people stood, sat and squatted, close-packed on the roof--and without exception they were Negroes! There were hundreds of them, and it was their low-voiced conversation which I had heard. But what held my gaze was that upon which their eyes were fixed.

About the center of the roof rose a sort of teocalli some ten feet high, almost exactly like those found in Mexico and on which the priests of the Aztecs sacrificed human victims. This, allowing for its infinitely smaller scale, was an exact type of those sacrificial pyramids. On the flat top of it was a curiously carved altar, and beside it stood a lank, dusky form whom even the ghastly mask he wore could not disguise to my gaze--Santiago, the Haiti voodoo fetish man. On the altar lay John Gordon, stripped to the waist and bound hand and foot, but conscious.

I reeled back from the roof edge, rent in twain by indecision. Even the stimulus of the elixir was not equal to this. Then a sound brought me about to see Hassim struggling dizzily to his knees. I reached him with two long strides and ruthlessly smashed him down again. Then I noticed a queer sort of contrivance dangling from his girdle. I bent and examined it. It was a mask similar to that worn by Santiago. Then my mind leaped swift and sudden to a wild desperate plan, which to my dope-ridden brain seemed not at all wild or desperate. I stepped softly to the tower and, opening the door, peered inward. I saw no one who might need to be silenced, but I saw a long silken robe hanging upon a peg in the wall. The luck of the dope fiend! I snatched it and closed the door again. Hassim showed no signs of consciousness but I gave him another smash on the chin to make sure and, seizing his mask, hurried to the ledge.

A low guttural chant floated up to me, jangling, barbaric, with an undertone of maniacal blood-lust. The Negroes, men and women, were swaying back and forth to the wild rhythm of their death chant. On the teocalli Santiago stood like a statue of black basalt, facing the east, dagger held high--a wild and terrible sight, naked as he was save for a wide silken girdle and that inhuman mask on his face. The moon thrust a red rim above the eastern horizon and a faint breeze stirred the great black plumes which nodded above the voodoo man's mask. The chant of the worshipers dropped to a low, sinister whisper.

I hurriedly slipped on the death mask, gathered the robe close about me and prepared for the descent. I was prepared to drop the full distance, being sure in the superb confidence of my insanity that I would land unhurt, but as I climbed over the ledge I found a steel ladder leading down. Evidently Hassim, one of the voodoo priests, intended descending this way. So down I went, and in haste, for I knew that the instant the moon's lower rim cleared the city's skyline, that motionless dagger would descend into Gordon's breast.

Gathering the robe close about me so as to conceal my white skin, I stepped down upon the roof and strode forward through rows of black worshipers who shrank aside to let me through. To the foot of the teocalli I stalked and up the stair that ran about it, until I stood beside the death altar and marked the dark red stains upon it. Gordon lay on his back, his eyes open, his face drawn and haggard, but his gaze dauntless and unflinching.

Santiago's eyes blazed at me through the slits of his mask, but I read no suspicion in his gaze until I reached forward and took the dagger from his hand. He was too much astonished to resist, and the black throng fell suddenly silent. That he saw my hand was not that of a Negro it is certain, but he was simply struck speechless with astonishment. Moving swiftly I cut Gordon's bonds and hauled him erect. Then Santiago with a shriek leaped upon me--shrieked again and, arms flung high, pitched headlong from the teocalli with his own dagger buried to the hilt in his breast.

Then the black worshipers were on us with a screech and a roar--leaping on the steps of the teocalli like black leopards in the moonlight, knives flashing, eyes gleaming whitely.

I tore mask and robe from me and answered Gordon's exclamation with a wild laugh. I had hoped that by virtue of my disguise I might get us both safely away but now I was content to die there at his side.

He tore a great metal ornament from the altar, and as the attackers came he wielded this. A moment we held them at bay and then they flowed over us like a black wave. This to me was Valhalla! Knives stung me and blackjacks smashed against me, but I laughed and drove my iron fists in straight, steam-hammer smashes that shattered flesh and bone. I saw Gordon's crude weapon rise and fall, and each time a man went down. Skulls shattered and blood splashed and the dark fury swept over me. Nightmare faces swirled about me and I was on my knees; up again and the faces crumpled before my blows. Through far mists I seemed to hear a hideous familiar voice raised in imperious command.

Gordon was swept away from me but from the sounds I knew that the work of death still went on. The stars reeled through fogs of blood, but Hell's exaltation was on me and I reveled in the dark tides of fury until a darker, deeper tide swept over me and I knew no more.

Chapter 20. Ancient Horror

"Here now in his triumph where all things falter,
Stretched out on the spoils that his own hand spread,
As a God self-slain on his own strange altar,
Death lies dead."
--Swinburne

Slowly I drifted back into life--slowly, slowly. A mist held me and in the mist I saw a Skull--

I lay in a steel cage like a captive wolf, and the bars were too strong, I saw, even for my strength. The cage seemed to be set in a sort of niche in the wall and I was looking into a large room. This room was under the earth, for the floor was of stone flags and the walls and ceiling were composed of gigantic block of the same material. Shelves ranged the walls, covered with weird appliances, apparently of a scientific nature, and more were on the great table that stood in the center of the room. Beside this sat Kathulos.

The sorcerer was clad in a snaky yellow robe, and those hideous hands and that terrible head were more pronouncedly reptilian than ever. He turned his great yellow eyes toward me, like pools of livid fire, and his parchment-thin lips moved in what probably passed for a smile.

I staggered erect and gripped the bars, cursing.

"Gordon, curse you, where is Gordon?"

Kathulos took a test-tube from the table, eyed it closely and emptied it into another.

"Ah, my friend awakes," he murmured in his voice--the voice of a living dead man.

He thrust his hands into his long sleeves and turned fully to me.

"I think in you," he said distinctly, "I have created a Frankenstein monster. I made of you a superhuman creature to serve my wishes and you broke from me. You are the bane of my might, worse than Gordon even. You have killed valuable servants and interfered with my plans. However, your evil comes to an end tonight. Your friend Gordon broke away but he is being hunted through the tunnels and cannot escape.

"You," he continued with the sincere interest of the scientist, "are a most interesting subject. Your brain must be formed differently from any other man that ever lived. I will make a close study of it and add it to my laboratory. How a man, with the apparent need of the elixir in his system, has managed to go on for two days still stimulated by the last draft is more than I can understand."

My heart leaped. With all his wisdom, little Zuleika had tricked him and he evidently did not know that she had filched a flask of the life-giving stuff from him.

"The last draft you had from me," he went on, "was sufficient only for some eight hours. I repeat, it has me puzzled. Can you offer any suggestion?"

I snarled wordlessly. He sighed.

"As always the barbarian. Truly the proverb speaks: 'Jest with the wounded tiger and warm the adder in your bosom before you seek to lift the savage from his savagery.'"

He meditated awhile in silence. I watched him uneasily. There was about him a vague and curious difference--his long fingers emerging from the sleeves drummed on the chair arms and some hidden exultation strummed at the back of his voice, lending it unaccustomed vibrancy.

"And you might have been a king of the new regime," he said suddenly. "Aye, the new--new and inhumanly old!"

I shuddered as his dry cackling laugh rasped out.

He bent his head as if listening. From far off seemed to come a hum of guttural voices. His lips writhed in a smile.

"My black children," he murmured. "They tear my enemy Gordon to pieces in the tunnels. They, Mr. Costigan, are my real henchmen and it was for their edification tonight that I laid John Gordon on the sacrificial stone. I would have preferred to have made some experiments with him, based on certain scientific theories, but my children must be humored. Later under my tutelage they will outgrow their childish superstitions and throw aside their foolish customs, but now they must be led gently by the hand.

"How do you like these under-the-earth corridors, Mr. Costigan?" he switched suddenly. "You thought of them--what? No doubt that the white savages of your Middle Ages built them? Faugh! These tunnels are older than your world! They were brought into being by mighty kings, too many eons ago for your mind to grasp, when an imperial city towered where this crude village of London stands. All trace of that metropolis has crumbled to dust and vanished, but these corridors were built by more than human skill--ha ha! Of all the teeming thousands who move daily above them, none knows of their existence save my servants--and not all of them. Zuleika, for instance, does not know of them, for of late I have begun to doubt her loyalty and shall doubtless soon make of her an example."

At that I hurled myself blindly against the side of the cage, a red wave of hate and fury tossing me in its grip. I seized the bars and strained until the veins stood out on my forehead and the muscles bulged and crackled in my arms and shoulders. And the bars bent before my onslaught--a little but no more, and finally the power flowed from my limbs and I sank down trembling and weakened. Kathulos watched me imperturbably.

"The bars hold," be announced with something almost like relief in his tone. "Frankly, I prefer to be on the opposite side of them. You are a human ape if there was ever one."

He laughed suddenly and wildly.

"But why do you seek to oppose me?" he shrieked unexpectedly. "Why defy me, who am Kathulos, the Sorcerer, great even in the days of the old empire? Today, invincible! A magician, a scientist, among ignorant savages! Ha ha!"

I shuddered, and sudden blinding light broke in on me. Kathulos himself was an addict, and was fired by the stuff of his choice! What hellish concoction was strong enough, terrible enough to thrill the Master and inflame him, I do not know, nor do I wish to know. Of all the uncanny knowledge that was his, I, knowing the man as I did, count this the most weird and grisly.

"You, you paltry fool!" he was ranting, his face lit supernaturally.

"Know you who I am? Kathulos of Egypt! Bah! They knew me in the old days! I reigned in the dim misty sea lands ages and ages before the sea rose and engulfed the land. I died, not as men die; the magic draft of life everlasting was ours! I drank deep and slept. Long I slept in my lacquered case! My flesh withered and grew hard; my blood dried in my veins. I became as one dead. But still within me burned the spirit of life, sleeping but anticipating the awakening. The great cities crumbled to dust. The sea drank the land. The tall shrines and the lofty spires sank beneath the green waves. All this I knew as I slept, as a man knows in dreams. Kathulos of Egypt? Faugh! *Kathulos of At-lantis* !"

I uttered a sudden involuntary cry. This was too grisly for sanity.

"Aye, the magician, the sorcerer.

"And down the long years of savagery, through which the barbaric races struggled to rise without their masters, the legend came of the day of empire, when one of the Old Race would rise up from the sea. Aye, and lead to victory the black people who were our slaves in the old days.

"These brown and yellow people, what care I for them? The blacks were the slaves of my race, and I am their god today. They will obey me. The yellow and the brown peoples are fools--I make them my tools and the day will come when my black warriors will turn on them and slay at my word. And you, you white barbarians, whose ape-ancestors forever defied my race and me, your doom is at hand! And when I mount my universal throne, the only whites shall be white slaves!

"The day came as prophesied, when my case, breaking free from the halls where it lay--where it had lain when Atlantis was still sovereign of the world--where since her empery it had sunk into the green fathoms--when my case, I say, was smitten by the deep sea tides and moved and stirred, and thrust aside the clinging seaweed that masks temples and minarets, and came floating up past the lofty sapphire and golden spires, up through the green waters, to float upon the lazy waves of the sea.

"Then came a white fool carrying out the destiny of which he was not aware. The men on his ship, true believers, knew that the time had come. And I--the air entered my nostrils and I awoke from the long, long sleep. I stirred and moved and lived. And rising in the night, I slew the fool that had lifted me from the ocean, and my servants made obeisance to me and took me into Africa, where I abode awhile and learned new languages and new ways of a new world and became strong.

"The wisdom of your dreary world--ha ha! I who delved deeper in the mysteries of the old than any man dared go! All that men know today, I know, and the knowledge beside that which I have brought down the centuries is as a grain of sand beside a mountain! You should know something of that knowledge! By it I lifted you from one hell to plunge you into a greater! You fool, here at my hand is that which would lift you from this! Aye, would strike from you the chains whereby I have bound you!"

He snatched up a golden vial and shook it before my gaze. I eyed it as men dying in the desert must eye the distant mirages. Kathulos fingered it meditatively. His unnatural excitement seemed to have passed suddenly, and when he spoke again it was in the passionless, measured tones of the scientist.

"That would indeed be an experiment worthwhile--to free you of the elixir habit and see if your dope-riddled body would sustain life. Nine times out of ten the victim, with the need and stimulus removed, would die--but you are such a giant of a brute--"

He sighed and set the vial down.

"The dreamer opposes the man of destiny. My time is not my own or I should choose to spend my life pent in my laboratories, carrying out my experiments. But now, as in the days of the old empire when kings sought my counsel, I must work and labor for the good of the race at large. Aye, I must toil and sow the seed of glory against the full coming of the imperial days when the seas give up all their living dead."

I shuddered. Kathulos laughed wildly again. His fingers began to drum his chair arms and his face gleamed with the unnatural light once more. The red visions had begun to seethe in his skull again.

"Under the green seas they lie, the ancient masters, in their lacquered cases, dead as men reckon death, but only sleeping. Sleeping through the long ages as hours, awaiting the day of awakening! The old masters, the wise men, who foresaw the day when the sea would gulp the land, and who made ready. Made ready that they might rise again in the barbaric days to come. As did I. Sleeping they lie, ancient kings and grim wizards, who died as men die, before Atlantis sank. Who, sleeping, sank with her but who shall arise again!

"Mine the glory! I rose first. And I sought out the site of old cities, on shores that did not sink. Vanished, long vanished. The barbarian tide swept over them thousands of years ago as the green waters swept over their elder sister of the deeps. On some, the deserts stretch bare. Over some, as here, young barbarian cities rise."

He halted suddenly. His eyes sought one of the dark openings that marked a corridor. I think his strange intuition warned him of some impending danger but I do not believe that he had any inkling of how dramatically our scene would be interrupted.

As he looked, swift footsteps sounded and a man appeared suddenly in the doorway--a man disheveled, tattered and bloody. John Gordon! Kathulos sprang erect with a cry, and Gordon, gasping as from superhuman exertion, brought down the revolver he held in his hand and fired point-blank. Kathulos staggered, clapping his hand to his breast, and then, groping wildly, reeled to the wall and fell against it. A doorway opened and he reeled through, but as Gordon leaped fiercely across the chamber, a blank stone surface met his gaze, which yielded not to his savage hammerings.

He whirled and ran drunkenly to the table where lay a bunch of keys the Master had dropped there.

"The vial!" I shrieked. "Take the vial!" And he thrust it into his pocket.

Back along the corridor through which he had come sounded a faint clamor growing swiftly like a wolf-pack in full cry. A few precious seconds spent with fumbling for the right key, then the cage door swung open and I sprang out. A sight for the gods we were, the two of us! Slashed, bruised and cut, our garments hanging in tatters--my wounds had ceased to bleed, but now as I moved they began again, and from the stiffness of my hands I knew that my knuckles were shattered. As for Gordon, he was fairly drenched in blood from crown to foot.

We made off down a passage in the opposite direction from the menacing noise, which I knew to be the black servants of the Master in full pursuit of us. Neither of us was in good shape for running, but we did our best. Where we were going I had no idea. My superhuman strength had deserted me and I was going now on willpower alone. We switched off into another corridor and we had not gone twenty steps until, looking back, I saw the first of the black devils round the corner.

A desperate effort increased our lead a trifle. But they had seen us, were in full view now, and a yell of fury broke from them to be succeeded by a more sinister silence as they bent all efforts to overhauling us.

There a short distance in front of us we saw a stair loom suddenly in the gloom. If we might reach that--but we saw something else.

Against the ceiling, between us and the stairs, hung a huge thing like an iron grille, with great spikes along the bottom--a portcullis. And even as we looked, without halting in our panting strides, it began to move.

"They're lowering the portcullis!" Gordon croaked, his blood-streaked face a mask of exhaustion and will.

Now the blacks were only ten feet behind us--now the huge grate, gaining momentum, with a creak of rusty, unused mechanism, rushed downward. A final spurt, a gasping straining nightmare of effort--and

Gordon, sweeping us both along in a wild burst of pure nerve-strength, hurled us under and through, and the grate crashed behind us!

A moment we lay gasping, not heeding the frenzied horde who raved and screamed on the other side of the grate. So close had that final leap been, that the great spikes in their descent had torn shreds from our clothing.

The blacks were thrusting at us with daggers through the bars, but we were out of reach and it seemed to me that I was content to lie there and die of exhaustion. But Gordon weaved unsteadily erect and hauled me with him.

"Got to get out," he croaked; "go to warn--Scotland Yard--honeycombs in heart of London--high explosives--arms--ammunition."

We blundered up the steps, and in front of us I seemed to hear a sound of metal grating against metal. The stairs ended abruptly, on a landing that terminated in a blank wall. Gordon hammered against this and the inevitable secret doorway opened. Light streamed in, through the bars of a sort of grille. Men in the uniform of London police were sawing at these with hacksaws, and even as they greeted us, an opening was made through which we crawled.

"You're hurt, sir!" One of the men took Gordon's arm.

My companion shook him off.

"There's no time to lose! Out of here, as quick as we can go!"

I saw that we were in a basement of some sort. We hastened up the steps and out into the early dawn which was turning the east scarlet. Over the tops of smaller houses I saw in the distance a great gaunt building on the roof of which, I felt instinctively, that wild drama had been enacted the night before.

"That building was leased some months ago by a mysterious Chinaman," said Gordon, following my gaze. "Office building originally--the neighborhood deteriorated and the building stood vacant for some time. The new tenant added several stories to it but left it apparently empty. Had my eye on it for some time."

This was told in Gordon's jerky swift manner as we started hurriedly along the sidewalk. I listened mechanically, like a man in a trance. My vitality was ebbing fast and I knew that I was going to crumple at any moment.

"The people living in the vicinity had been reporting strange sights and noises. The man who owned the basement we just left heard queer sounds emanating from the wall of the basement and called the police. About that time I was racing back and forth among those cursed corridors like a hunted rat and I heard the police banging on the wall. I found the secret door and opened it but found it barred by a grating. It was while I was telling the astounded policemen to procure a hacksaw that the pursuing Negroes, whom I had eluded for the moment, came into sight and I was forced to shut the door and run for it again. By pure luck I found you and by pure luck managed to find the way back to the door.

"Now we must get to Scotland Yard. If we strike swiftly, we may capture the entire band of devils. Whether I killed Kathulos or not I do not know, or if he can be killed by mortal weapons. But to the best of my knowledge all of them are now in those subterranean corridors and--"

At that moment the world shook! A brain-shattering roar seemed to break the sky with its incredible detonation; houses tottered and crashed to ruins; a mighty pillar of smoke and flame burst from the earth and on its wings great masses of debris soared skyward. A black fog of smoke and dust and falling timbers enveloped the world, a pro-longed thunder seemed to rumble up from the center of the earth as of walls and ceilings falling, and amid the uproar and the screaming I sank down and knew no more.

Chapter 21. *The Breaking of the Chain/*

"And like a soul belated,
In heaven and hell unmated;
By cloud and mist abated;
Come out of darkness morn."
--Swinburne

There is little need to linger on the scenes of horror of that terrible London morning. The world is familiar with and knows most of the details attendant to the great explosion which wiped out a tenth of that great city with a resultant loss of lives and property. For such a happening some reason must needs be given; the tale of the deserted building got out, and many wild stories were circulated. Finally, to still the rumors, the report was unofficially given out that this building had been the rendezvous and secret stronghold of a gang of international anarchists, who had stored its basement full of high explosives and who had supposedly ignited these accidentally. In a way there was a good deal to this tale, as you know, but the threat that had lurked there far transcended any anarchist.

All this was told to me, for when I sank unconscious, Gordon, attributing my condition to exhaustion and a need of the hashish to the use of which he thought I was addicted, lifted me and with the aid of the stunned policemen got me to his rooms before returning to the scene of the explosion. At his rooms he found Hansen, and Zuleika handcuffed to the bed as I had left her. He released her and left her to tend to me, for all London was in a terrible turmoil and he was needed elsewhere.

When I came to myself at last, I looked up into her starry eyes and lay quiet, smiling up at her. She sank down upon my bosom, nestling my head in her arms and covering my face with her kisses.

"Steephen!" she sobbed over and over, as her tears splashed hot on my face.

I was scarcely strong enough to put my arms about her but I managed it, and we lay there for a space, in silence, except for the girl's hard, racking sobs.

"Zuleika, I love you," I murmured.

"And I love you, Steephen," she sobbed. "Oh, it is so hard to part now--but I'm going with you, Steephen; I can't live without you!"

"My dear child," said John Gordon, entering the room suddenly, "Costigan's not going to die. We will let him have enough hashish to tide him along, and when he is stronger we will take him off the habit slowly."

"You don't understand, sahib; it is not hashish Steephen must have. It is something which only the Master knew, and now that he is dead or is fled, Steephen cannot get it and must die."

Gordon shot a quick, uncertain glance at me. His fine face was drawn and haggard, his clothes sooty and torn from his work among the debris of the explosion.

"She's right, Gordon," I said languidly. "I'm dying. Kathulos killed the hashish-craving with a concoction he called the elixir. I've been keeping myself alive on some of the stuff that Zuleika stole from him and gave me, but I drank it all last night."

I was aware of no craving of any kind, no physical or mental discomfort even. All my mechanism was slowing down fast; I had passed the stage where the need of the elixir would tear and rend me. I felt only a great lassitude and a desire to sleep. And I knew that the moment I closed my eyes, I would die.

"A strange dope, that elixir," I said with growing languor. "It burns and freezes and then at last the craving kills easily and without torment."

"Costigan, curse it," said Gordon desperately, "you can't go like this! That vial I took from the Egyptian's table--what is in it?"

"The Master swore it would free me of my curse and probably kill me also," I muttered. "I'd forgotten about it. Let me have it; it can no more than kill me and I'm dying now."

"Yes, quick, let me have it!" exclaimed Zuleika fiercely, springing to Gordon's side, her hands passionately outstretched. She returned with the vial which he had taken from his pocket, and knelt beside me, holding it to my lips, while she murmured to me gently and soothingly in her own language.

I drank, draining the vial, but feeling little interest in the whole matter. My outlook was purely impersonal, at such a low ebb was my life, and I cannot even remember how the stuff tasted. I only remember feeling a curious sluggish fire burn faintly along my veins, and the last thing I saw was Zuleika crouching over me, her great eyes fixed with a burning intensity on me. Her tense little hand rested inside her blouse, and remembering her vow to take her own life if I died I tried to lift a hand and disarm her, tried to tell Gordon to take away the dagger she had hidden in her garments. But speech and action failed me and I drifted away into a curious sea of unconsciousness.

Of that period I remember nothing. No sensation fired my sleeping brain to such an extent as to bridge the gulf over which I drifted. They say I lay like a dead man for hours, scarcely breathing, while Zuleika hovered over me, never leaving my side an instant, and fighting like a tigress when anyone tried to coax her away to rest. Her chain was broken.

As I had carried the vision of her into that dim land of nothingness, so her dear eyes were the first thing which greeted my returning consciousness. I was aware of a greater weakness than I thought possible for a man to feel, as if I had been an invalid for months, but the life in me, faint though it was, was sound and normal, caused by no artificial stimulation. I smiled up at my girl and murmured weakly:

"Throw away your dagger, little Zuleika; I'm going to live."

She screamed and fell on her knees beside me, weeping and laughing at the same time. Women are strange beings, of mixed and powerful emotions, truly.

Gordon entered and grasped the hand which I could not lift from the bed.

"You're a case for an ordinary human physician now, Costigan," he said. "Even a layman like myself can tell that. For the first time since I've known you, the look in your eyes is entirely sane. You look like a man who has had a complete nervous breakdown, and needs about a year of rest and quiet. Great heavens, man, you've been through enough, outside your dope experience, to last you a lifetime."

"Tell me first," said I, "was Kathulos killed in the explosion?"

"I don't know," answered Gordon somberly. "Apparently the entire system of subterranean passages was destroyed. I know my last bullet--the last bullet that was in the revolver which I wrested from one of my attackers--found its mark in the Master's body, but whether he died from the wound, or whether a bullet can hurt him, I do not know. And whether in his death agonies he ignited the tons and tons of high explosives which were stored in the corridors, or whether the Negroes did it unintentionally, we shall never know.

"My God, Costigan, did you ever see such a honeycomb? And we know not how many miles in either direction the passages reached. Even now Scotland Yard men are combing the subways and basements of the town for secret openings. All known openings, such as the one through which we came and the one in Soho 48, were blocked by falling walls. The office building was simply blown to atoms."

"What about the men who raided Soho 48?"

"The door in the library wall had been closed. They found the Chinaman you killed, but searched the house without avail. Lucky for them, too, else they had doubtless been in the tunnels when the explosion came, and perished with the hundreds of Negroes who must have died then."

"Every Negro in London must have been there."

"I dare say. Most of them are voodoo worshipers at heart and the power the Master wielded was incredible. They died, but what of him? Was he blown to atoms by the stuff which he had secretly stored, or crushed when the stone walls crumbled and the ceilings came thundering down?"

"There is no way to search among those subterranean ruins, I suppose?"

"None whatever. When the walls caved in, the tons of earth upheld by the ceilings also came crashing down, filling the corridors with dirt and broken stone, blocking them forever. And on the surface of the earth, the houses which the vibration shook down were heaped high in utter ruins. What happened in those terrible corridors must remain forever a mystery."

My tale draws to a close. The months that followed passed uneventfully, except for the growing happiness which to me was paradise, but which would bore you were I to relate it. But one day Gordon and I again discussed the mysterious happenings that had had their being under the grim hand of the Master.

"Since that day," said Gordon, "the world has been quiet. Africa has subsided and the East seems to have returned to her ancient sleep. There can be but one answer--living or dead, Kathulos was destroyed that morning when his world crashed about him."

"Gordon," said I, "what is the answer to that greatest of all mysteries?"

My friend shrugged his shoulders.

"I have come to believe that mankind eternally hovers on the brinks of secret oceans of which it knows nothing. Races have lived and vanished before our race rose out of the slime of the primitive, and it is likely still others will live upon the earth after ours has vanished. Scientists have long upheld the theory that the Atlanteans possessed a higher civilization than our own, and on very different lines. Certainly Kathulos himself was proof that our boasted culture and knowledge were nothing beside that of whatever fearful civilization produced him.

"His dealings with you alone have puzzled all the scientific world, for none of them has been able to explain how he could remove the hashish craving, stimulate you with a drug so infinitely more powerful, and then produce another drug which entirely effaced the effects of the other."

"I have him to thank for two things," I said slowly; "the regaining of my lost manhood--and Zuleika. Kathulos, then, is dead, as far as any mortal thing can die. But what of those others--those 'ancient masters' who still sleep in the sea?"

Gordon shuddered.

"As I said, perhaps mankind loiters on the brink of unthinkable chasms of horror. But a fleet of gunboats is even now patrolling the oceans unobtrusively, with orders to destroy instantly any strange case that may be found floating--to destroy it and its contents. And if my word has any weight with the English government and the nations of the world, the seas will be so patrolled until doomsday shall let down the curtain on the races of today."

"At night I dream of them, sometimes," I muttered, "sleeping in their lacquered cases, which drip with strange seaweed, far down among the green surges--where unholy spires and strange towers rise in the dark ocean."

"We have been face to face with an ancient horror," said Gordon somberly, "with a fear too dark and mysterious for the human brain to cope with. Fortune has been with us; she may not again favor the sons of men. It is best that we be ever on our guard. The universe was not made for humanity alone; life takes strange phases and it is the first instinct of nature for the different species to destroy each other. No doubt we seemed as horrible to the Master as he did to us. We have scarcely tapped the chest of secrets which nature has stored, and I shudder to think of what that chest may hold for the human race."

"That's true," said I, inwardly rejoicing at the vigor which was beginning to course through my wasted veins, "but men will meet obstacles as they come, as men have always risen to meet them. Now, I am beginning to know the full worth of life and love, and not all the devils from all the abysses can hold me."

Gordon smiled.

"You have it coming to you, old comrade. The best thing is to forget all that dark interlude, for in that course lies light and happiness."

Black Wind Blowing

Chapter I - "I Take This Woman!"

Emmett Glanton jammed on the brakes of his old Model T and skidded to a squealing stop within a few feet of the apparition that had materialized out of the black, gusty night.

"What the Hell do you mean by jumping in front of my car like that?" he yelled wrathfully, recognizing the figure that posed grotesquely in the glare of the headlights. It was Joshua, the lumbering halfwit who worked for old John Bruckman; but Joshua in a mood such as Glanton had never seen before. In the white glare of the lights the fellow's broad brutish face was convulsed; foam flecked his lips and his eyes were red as those of a rabid wolf. He brandished his arms and croaked incoherently. Impressed, Glanton opened the door and stepped out of the car. On his feet he was inches taller than Joshua, but his rangy, broad-shouldered frame did not look impressive compared to the stooped, apish bulk of the halfwit.

There was menace in Joshua's mien. Gone was the dull, apathetic expression he usually wore. He bared his teeth and snarled like a wild beast as he rolled toward Glanton.

"Keep away from me, blast you!" Glanton warned. "What's the matter with you, anyway?"

"You're goin' over there!" mouthed the halfwit, gesturing vaguely southward. "Old John called you over the phone. I heered him!"

"Yes, he did," answered Glanton. "Asked me to come over as quick as I could. Didn't say why. What about it? You want to ride back with me?"

Joshua jumped up and down and battered his hairy breast like an ape with his splay fists. He gnashed his teeth and howled. Glanton's flesh crawled a little. It was black night, with the wind howling under a black sky, whipping the mesquite. And there in that little spot of light that apish figure cavorted and raved like a witch's familiar summoned up from Hell.

"I don't want to ride with you!" bellowed Joshua. "You ain't goin' there! I'll kill you if you try to go! I'll twist your head off with my hands!" He spread his great fingers and worked them like the hairy legs of great spiders before Glanton's face. Glanton bristled at the threat.

"What are you raving about?" he demanded. "I don't know why Bruckman called me, but--"

"I know!" howled Joshua, froth flying from his loose, working lips. "I listened outside the winder! You can't have her! I want her!"

"Want who?" Glanton was bewildered. This was mystery piled on mystery. Black, howling night, and old John Bruckman's voice shrieking over the party line, edged with frenzy, begging and demanding that his neighbor come to him as quickly as his car could get him there; then the wild drive over the wind-lashed road, and now this lunatic prancing in the glare of the headlights and mouthing bloody threats.

Joshua ignored his question. He seemed to have lost what little sense he had ever had. He was acting like a homicidal maniac. And through the rents in his ragged shirt bulged muscles capable of rending the average man limb from limb.

"I never seen one I wanted before!" he screamed. "But I want her! Old John don't want her! I heered him say so! If you didn't come maybe he'd give her to me! You go on back home or I'll kill you! I'll twist your head off and feed it to the buzzards! You think I'm just a harmless big fool, I bet!"

Grotesquely his bellowing voice rose to a high-pitched squeal.

"Well, if it'll satisfy you," said Glanton, watching him warily, "I've always thought you were dangerous. Bruckman's a fool to keep you on the ranch. I've expected you to go clean crazy and kill him some time."

"I ain't goin' to kill John," howled Joshua. "I'm goin' to kill you. You won't be the first, neither. I killed my brother Jake. He beat me once too often. I beat his head to jelly with a rock and dragged the body down the canyon and throwed it into the pool below the rapids!"

A maniacal glee convulsed his face as he screamed his hideous secret to the night, and his eyes looked like nothing this side of Hell.

"So that's what became of Jake! I always wondered why he disappeared and you came to live with old John. Couldn't stay in your shack in that lonely canyon after you killed him, eh?"

A momentary gleam of fear shot the murk of the maniac's eyes.

"He wouldn't stay in the pool," muttered Joshua. "He used to come back and scratch at the winder, with his head all bloody. I'd wake up at night and see him lookin' in at me and gaspin' and gurglin' tryin' to talk through the blood in his throat.

"But you won't come back and ha'nt me!" he shrieked suddenly, beginning to sway from side to side like a bull about to charge. "I'll spike you down with a stake and weight you down with rocks! I'll--" In the midst of his tirade he lunged suddenly at Glanton.

Glanton knew that if those huge arms ever locked about him his spine would snap like a stick. But he knew, too, that nine times out of ten a maniac will try to reach his victim's throat with his teeth. Joshua was no exception.

Reverting completely to the beast, he plunged in with his arms groping vaguely, and his jaws thrust out like a wolf's muzzle, slavering teeth bared in the glare of the headlights. Glanton stepped inside those waving arms and smashed his right fist against the out-jutting jaw with all his power. It would have stretched another man senseless. It stopped the halfwit in his tracks, and blood spurted.

Before he could recover his balance Glanton struck again and again, raining terrific blows to face and head, driving Joshua reeling and staggering before him. It was like beating a bull, but the ceaseless smashes kept the maniac off balance, confused and dazed him, kept him on the defensive.

Glanton was beginning to tire, and he wondered desperately what the end would be. The moment his blows began weakening Joshua would shake off his bewilderment and lunge to the attack again--

Abruptly they were out of the range of the car lights, and floundering in darkness. In panic lest the maniac should find his throat in the blackness, Glanton swung blindly and desperately, connected glancingly and felt his man fall away from him.

He stumbled himself and went on all fours, almost pitching down the slope that fell away beneath him. Crouching there he heard the sounds of Joshua's thundering fall down the slant. Glanton knew where he was now, knew that a few yards from the road the ground fell away in a steep slope a hundred feet long. It was not hard to navigate by daylight, but by night a man might take a nasty tumble and hurt himself badly on the broken rocks at the bottom. And Joshua, knocked over the edge by Glanton's last wild haymaker, was taking that tumble.

It might have been an animal falling down the slope, from the grunts and howls that welled up from below, but presently, when the rattle of pebbles and the sounds of a heavy rolling body had ceased, there was silence, and Glanton wondered if the lunatic lay senseless or dead at the bottom of the slope.

He called, but there was no answer. Then a sudden shudder shook him. Joshua might be creeping back up the slope in utter silence, this time maybe with a rock in his hand, such a rock as he had used to batter his brother Jake's head into a crimson pulp--

Glanton's eyes were getting accustomed to the darkness and he could make out the vague forms of black ridges, boulders and trees. The devil-begotten wind that shrieked through the trees would drown a stealthy footstep. When a man turns his back on peril it assumes an aspect of thousand-fold horror.

When Glanton started back to the car his flesh crawled cold, and at each step he expected to feel a frightful form land on his back, gnashing and tearing. It was with a gasp of relief that he lunged into the car, eased off the hand-brake, and clattered off down the dim road.

He was leaving Joshua behind him, alive or dead, and such was the grim magic of the gusty dark that at the moment he feared Joshua dead no less than Joshua living.

He heaved another sigh of relief when the red spot that was the light of John Bruckman's house began to glow in the black curtain ahead of him. He disliked Bruckman, but the old skinflint was sane at least, and any sane company was welcome after his experience with a brutish maniac in the black heart of this evil night.

A car stood before Bruckman's gate and Glanton recognized it as the one belonging to Lem Richards, justice of the peace in Skurlock, the little village which lay a few miles south of the Bruckman ranch.

Glanton knocked on the door and Bruckman's voice, with a strange, unnatural quaver in it, shouted:

"Who's there? Speak quick, or I'll shoot through the door!"

"It's me, Glanton!" called the ranchman in a hurry. "You asked me to come, didn't you?"

Chains rattled, a key grated in the lock, and the door swung inward. The black night seemed to flow in after Glanton with the wind that made the lamp flicker and the shadows dance along the walls, and Bruckman moaned and slammed the door in its ebon face. He jammed bolt and chain with trembling hands.

"Your confounded hired hand tried to kill me on the way over," Glanton began angrily. "I've told you that lunatic would go bad some day--"

He stopped short. Two other people were in the room. One was Lem Richards, the justice of the peace, a short, stolid, unimaginative man who sat before the hearth placidly chewing his quid.

The other was a girl, and at the sight of her a sort of shock passed over Emmett Glanton, bringing a sudden realization of his work-hardened hands and hickory shirt and rusty boots. She was like a breath of perfume from the world of tinsel and bright lights and evening gowns that he had almost forgotten in his toil to build up his fortune in this primitive country.

Her supple young figure was set off to its best advantage by the neat but costly dress she wore. Her loveliness dazzled Glanton at first glance; then he looked again and was appalled. For she was white and cold as a statue of marble, and her dilated eyes stared at him as though she had just seen a serpent writhe through the door.

"Oh, excuse me!" he said awkwardly, dragging off, his battered Stetson. "I wouldn't have come busting in here like this if I'd known there was a lady--"

"Never mind that!" snapped John Bruckman. He faced Glanton across the table, his face limned in the lamp-light. It was a haggard face, and in the burning eyes Glanton saw fear, murky bestial fear that made the man repulsive. Bruckman spoke hurriedly, the words tumbling over each other, and from time to time he glanced at the big clock on the mantel sullenly ticking off the seconds.

"Glanton, I hold a mortgage on your ranch, and it's due in a few days. Do you think you can meet your payment?"

Glanton felt like cursing the man. Had he called him over that windswept road on a night like this to discuss a mortgage? A glance at the white, tense girl told him something else was behind all this.

"I reckon I can," he said shortly. "I'm getting by--or would if you'd stay off my back long enough for me to get a start."

"I'll do that!" Bruckman's hands were shaking as he fumbled in his coat. "Look here! Here's the mortgage!" He tossed a document on the table. "And a thousand dollars in cash!" A compact bundle of bank notes plopped down on the table before Glanton's astounded eyes. "It's all yours--mortgage and money--if you'll do one thing for me!"

"And what's that?"

Bruckman's bony forefinger stabbed at the cringing girl.

"Marry her!"

"What?" Glanton wheeled and stared at her with a new intensity, and she stared wildly back, in evident fright, and bewilderment.

"Marry her?" He ran a hand dazedly across his head, vividly aware of the loneliness of the life he had been leading for the past three years.

"What does the young lady think about it?" he asked.

Bruckman snarled impatiently.

"What does it matter what she thinks? She's my niece, my ward. She'll do as I say. She could do worse than marry you. You're no common ridge-runner. You're a gentleman by birth and breeding--"

"Never mind that," growled Glanton, waving him aside. He stepped toward the girl.

"Are you willing to marry me?" he asked directly.

She looked full into his eyes for a long moment, with a desperate and pitiful intensity in her gaze. She must have read kindness and honesty there, for suddenly, impulsively, she sprang forward and caught his brown hand in both of hers, crying:

"Yes! Yes! *Please* marry me! Marry me and take me away from *him*--" Her gesture toward John Bruckman was one of fear and loathing, but the old man did not heed. He was staring fearfully at the clock again.

He clapped his hands in a spasm of nervousness.

"Quick! Quick! Lem brought the license, according to my instructions. He'll marry you now--now! Stand over here by the table and join hands."

Richards rose heavily and lumbered over to the table, fingering his worn book. All this drama and mystery meant nothing to him, except that another couple were to be married.

And so Emmett Glanton found himself standing holding the quivering hand of a girl he had never seen before, while the justice of the peace mumbled the ritual which made them husband and wife. And only then did he learn the girl's name--Joan Zukor.

"Do you, Emmett, take this woman..." droned the monotonous voice.

Glanton gave his reply mechanically, his fingers involuntarily clenching on the slim fingers they grasped. For, pressed briefly against a window, he had seen a face--a white, blood-streaked mask of murder--the face of the halfwit Joshua.

The maniac's eyes burned on Glanton with a mad hate, and on the woman at his side with a sickening flame of desire. Then the face was gone and the window framed only the blackness of the night.

None but Glanton had seen the lunatic. Richards, paid by old John, lumbered stolidly forth and the door shut behind him. Glanton and the girl stood looking at each other speechlessly, in sudden self-consciousness, but old John gave them no pause. He glared at the clock again, which showed ten minutes after eleven, jammed the mortgage and the bank notes into Glanton's hand and pushed him and the girl toward the door. Sweat dripped from his livid face, but a sort of wild triumph mingled with his strange fear.

"Get out! Get off my place! Take your wife and go! I wash my hands of her! I am no longer responsible for her! She's your burden! Go--and go quick!"

Chapter II - "Tell Them--In Pity's Name"

In a sort of daze Glanton found himself out on the porch with the girl, and from inside came the sound of drawn bolts and hooked chains. Angrily he took a step toward the door, then noticed the girl shivering beside him, huddling about her a cloak she had snatched as they were evicted.

"Come on, Joan," he said awkwardly, taking her arm. "I think your uncle must be crazy. We'd better go."

He felt her shudder.

"Yes, let us go quickly."

Richards, characteristically, had left the yard gate unfastened. It was flapping and banging in the wind which moaned through the junipers. Glanton groped his way toward the sound, sheltering the cowering girl against the gusts that whipped her cloak about her.

He shivered at the thick-set, cone-shaped outlines of the junipers along the walk. Either of them might be hiding the maniac who had glared through the window. The creature was no longer human; he was a beast of prey, ranging the night.

John Bruckman had given Glanton no chance to warn him of the madman. But Glanton decided he would phone back from his ranch house. They could not loiter there in the darkness, with that skulking fiend abroad.

He half expected to find Joshua crouching in the car, but it was empty, and a feeling of relief flooded him as he turned on the lights and their twin beams lanced the dark. The girl beside him sighed too, though she knew nothing of the death that lurked near them. But she sensed the evil of the night, the menace of the crowding blackness. Even such a dim illumination as this was comforting.

Wordless, Glanton started the car and they began the bumping, jolting ride. He was consumed with curiosity, but hesitated to put the question that itched on his tongue. Presently the girl herself spoke.

"You wonder why my uncle sold me like a slave--or an animal!"

"Don't say that!" exclaimed Glanton in quick sympathy. "You need not--"

"Why *shouldn't* you wonder?" she retorted bitterly. "I can only say--I don't know. He's my only relative, as far as I know. I've seen him only a few times in my life. Ever since I was a small child I've lived in boarding schools and I always understood he was supplying the money that lodged, dressed and educated me. But he seldom wrote; hardly ever visited me.

"I was in a school in Houston when I received a wire from my uncle ordering me to come to him at once. I came on the train to Skurlock, and arrived about nine tonight. Mr. Richards met me at the station. He told me that my uncle had phoned and asked him to drive me out to his ranch. He had the license with him, though I didn't know it at the time.

"When we got here my uncle told me abruptly that I'd have to marry a young man he had sent for. Naturally, I--I was terrified--" She faltered and then laid a timid hand on his arm. "I was afraid--I didn't know what kind of a man it might be."

"I'll be a good husband to you, girl," he said awkwardly, and thrilled with pleasure at the sincerity in her tone as she replied:

"I know it. You have kind eyes and gentle hands. Strong, but gentle."

They were approaching a place where the road had been straightened by a new track, which, instead of swinging wide around the sloping edge of a steep, thicket-grown knoll, crossed a shallow ravine by a crude bridge and ran close by the knob on the opposite side, where it sheered off in a forty-foot cliff.

As the knoll grew dimly out of the windy darkness ahead of them, a grisly premonition rose in Glanton's breast. Joshua, loping through the mesquite like a lobo wolf, could have reached that knob ahead of them. It was the most logical place along the road for an ambush. A man crouching on the thicket-clad crest of the cliff could hurl a boulder down on a car passing along the new stretch of road--

With sudden decision, Glanton wrenched the car into the old track, now a faint trace grown up in broom weeds and prickly pears.

Joan caught at him for support as she was thrown from side to side by the jouncing of the auto. Then as they swung around the slope and came back into the plain road again, behind and above them yammered a fiendish howling--the maddened, primordial shrieking of a baffled beast of prey which realizes that his victims have eluded him.

"What's that?" gasped Joan, clutching at Glanton.

"Just a bobcat squalling in the brush on that knob," he assured her, but it was with convulsive haste that he jammed his foot down on the accelerator and sent the car thundering down the road. Tomorrow, he swore, he'd raise a posse and hunt down that slavering human beast as he would a rabid coyote.

He could imagine the madman loping along the road after them, foam from his bared fangs dripping onto his bare, hairy breast. He was glad the lamp was burning in the parlor of his ranch house. It reached a warm shaft of light to them across the windy reaches of the night.

He did not drive the car into the shed that served as garage. He drove it as close to the porch as he could get it, and opened the car door in the light that streamed from the house, as old Juan Sanchez, his Mexican man-of-all-work, opened the front door.

Glanton was briefly aware of the bareness of his residence. There had been no time to adorn it in his toil to build his spread. But now he must have a front yard with a fence around it and some rose bushes and spineless decorative cacti. Women liked things like that.

"This is my wife, Sanchez," he said briefly. "Senora Joan."

The old Mexican hid his astonishment with a low bow, and said, with the natural courtliness of his race:

"Buenas noches, senora! Welcome to the *hacienda."*

In the parlor Glanton said: "Sit down by the fire and warm yourself, Joan. It's been a cold drive. Sanchez, stir up the fire and throw on some more mesquite chunks. I'm going to call up John Bruckman. There's something he ought to know--"

But even as he reached for the phone the bell jangled discordantly. As he lifted the receiver over the line came John Bruckman's voice, brittle with fear and more than fear--with physical agony.

"Emmett! Emmett Glanton! Tell them--in pity's name tell them that you've married Joan Zukor! Tell them I'm no longer responsible for her!"

"Tell who?" demanded Glanton, all but speechless with amazement.

Joan was on her feet, white-faced; that frantic voice shrieking from the receiver had reached her ears.

"These devils!" squalled the voice of John Bruckman. "The Black Brothers of--aaagh--Mercy!"

The voice broke in a loud shriek, and in the brief silence that followed there sounded a low, gurgling, indescribably repellent laugh. And Glanton's hair stood up, for he knew it was not John Bruckman who laughed.

"Hello!" he yelled. "John! John Bruckman!"

There was no answer. A click told him that the receiver had been hung up at the other end, and a grisly conviction shook him that it had not been John Bruckman's hand who had hung it up.

He turned to the girl, who stood silent and wide-eyed in the middle of the room, as he snatched a gun from its scabbard hanging on the wall.

"I've got to go back to Bruckman's ranch," he said. "Something devilish is happening over there, and the old man seems to need help bad."

She was speechless. Impulsively he took her hands in his and stroked them reassuringly.

"Don't be afraid, kid," he said. "Sanchez will take care of you till I get back. And I won't be gone long."

Chapter III - Dead Madness

As he drew the old Mexican out onto the porch a glance back showed her still standing dumbly in the center of the room, her hands pressed childishly to her breasts, an image of youthful fright and bewilderment lost in an unfamiliar world of violence and horror.

"I don't know what the Hell's happened over at Bruckman's," he said swiftly and low-voiced to Sanchez. "But be careful. Joshua, the halfwit's gone on the rampage. He tried to kill me tonight, and he laid for us at the knob where the new road passes. Probably meant to brain me with a rock and kidnap Joan. Shoot him like a coyote if he shows his head on this ranch while I'm gone."

"Trust me, *senor!*" Old Sanchez's face was grim as he fondled the worn butt of his old single-action Colt. Men had died before that black muzzle in the wild old days when Sanchez had ridden with Pancho Villa. Sanchez could be depended on. Glanton clapped him on the back, leaped into the Ford and roared away southward.

The road before him was a white crack in a black wall, opening steadily in the glare of the headlights. He drove recklessly, half expecting each moment to see the shambling figure of the maniac spring out of the blackness. Grimly he touched the butt of the pistol thrust into the waistband of his trousers.

Aversion to driving under that gloomy cliff was so strong in Glanton that again he swung aside and followed the dimmer, longer road that wound around the opposite side of the knob.

And as he did so he was aware of another roar, above that of his own racing motor. He caught the reflection of powerful headlights. Some other car was eating up the road, racing northward and taking the shorter cut. As he drove into the open road beyond the knob he looked back and glimpsed a rapidly receding tail-light. A nameless foreboding seized him, urging him to wheel around and race back to his own ranch.

But there was not necessarily anything sinister in a car speeding northward even at that hour. It was probably some ranchman who lived north of Glanton returning home from Skurlock, or some traveling salesman bound for one of the little cow towns still further north, and leaving the paved highways to take a short cut.

There was no light in the window of the Bruckman ranch house as Glanton approached it; only the glow of the fire in the fireplace staining the windows with lurid blood, crimsoning it without illuminating. There was no sound but the moaning of the ghostly wind through the dark junipers as Glanton went up the walk. But the front door stood open.

Pistol in hand, Glanton peered in. He caught the glimmer of red coals glowing on the hearth. The dry, toneless ticking of the clock made him start nervously.

He called: "John! John Bruckman!"

No answer, but somewhere a moan rose in the fire-shadowed darkness, a low, whimpering of anguish, thick and gurgling as if through a gag of welling blood. And a steady drip, drip of something wet and sticky on the floor.

Panic clawed at Glanton's spine as he moved toward the smoldering hearth, instinct drawing him toward the one spot of light in the room. At the moment he did not remember just where stood the table with the oil lamp on it. He must have a moment to gather his wits, to locate it.

He groped for a match, then froze in his tracks. A black hand had materialized out of the shadows, faintly revealed in the light of the glowing embers. It cast something on the coals while Glanton stood transfixed.

Little tongues of red grew to life; the fire rose and the shadows retreated before the widening pool of wavering light. A face grew out of the darkness before Emmett Glanton--a grinning face that was like a carven mask somehow imbued with evil life. White pointed teeth reflected the firelight, eyes red as the eyes of an owl burned at him.

With a choking cry Glanton lifted his gun and fired full at the face. At that range he could not miss. The face vanished with a shattering crash and Glanton was showered with tiny particles that stung his hand.

But a low laugh rang through the room--the laugh he had heard over the phone! Whence it came he could not be sure, but in the flash of intuition that came to him, as it often comes to men in desperate straits, he realized the trick that had been played upon him, and wheeled with a gasp of pure terror. Pointblank he fired, with the muzzle jammed against the bulk that was almost on him--the bulk of the fiend that had crept up *behind him while he was staring at its reflection in front of him.*

There was an agonized grunt and something that swished venomously ripped away the front of his shirt. And then the monster was down and floundering in its death throes in the shadows at his feet, and in a panic Glanton fired down at it again and again, until its thrashing ceased and in the deafening silence that followed the booming of the shots he heard only the dry tick-tock of the clock, the drip-drip on the floor and the moaning that rose eerily in the gruesome dark.

His hands were clammy with sweat when he found the oil lamp and lighted it. As the flame sprang up, sending the shadows slinking back to the corners, he glared fearfully at the thing sprawled before the hearth. At least it was a *man*--a tall, powerful man, naked to the waist, his shoulders and arching chest gigantic, his arms thick with knotting muscles.

Blood oozed from three wounds in that massive torso. He was black, but he was not a Negro. He seemed to be stained with some sort of paint from his shaven crown to his fingertips. And the fingers of one hand were frightfully armed, with steel hooks that were hollow nearly to the points and slipped over the fingers, curving and razor sharp, making terrible, tiger-like talons.

The thick lips, drawn back, revealed teeth filed to points, and then Glanton saw that he was not painted all over, after all. In the center of the breast a circle of white skin showed, and inside that circle there was a strange black symbol; it looked like a blind, black face.

An arrangement of mirrors fastened at right angles to the mantel and to the wall, one shattered by his bullet, revealed the trick by which he meant to take Glanton off guard. He must have made his arrangements, simple and easy enough, when he heard the car driving up. But it was diabolical, betraying a twisted mind.

From where he had been standing, Glanton could not see his own reflection in the mirror on the mantel, but only the reflection of the black man behind and to one side of him, like a spectral face floating in the shadows.

What takes long in the telling flashed lightning-like through Glanton's mind as he looked down at the black man; and then he saw something else. He saw old John Bruckman.

The old man lay naked on a table, on his back, arms and legs spread wide, so that his body formed a St. Andrew's Cross. Through each hand, nailing it to the wood, and through each ankle, a black spike had been driven.

His tongue had been pulled out of his mouth and a steel skewer was driven through it. A ghastly raw, red patch showed on his breast, where a portion of skin as big as a man's palm had been savagely sliced away. And that piece of skin lay on the table beside him and Glanton gasped at the sight of it. For it bore the same unholy symbol that showed on the breast of the dead man by the hearth. Blood trickled along the table, dripped on the floor.

Nauseated, Glanton drew forth the skewer from John Bruckman's tongue. Bruckman gagged, spat forth a great mouthful of blood and made incoherent sounds.

"Take it easy, John," said Glanton. "I'll get some pliers and pull these spikes out--"

"Let them be!" gurgled Bruckman, scarcely intelligible with his butchered tongue. "They're barbed--you'll tear my hands off. I'm dying--they hurt me in ways that don't show so plainly. Let me die in as little pain as possible. Sorry--would have warned you *he* was waiting for you in the dark--but this accursed skewer--couldn't even scream. He heard your car and made ready--mirrors--always carry their paraphernalia with them--paraphernalia of illusion--deception and murder! Whiskey, quick! On that shelf!"

Though he winced at the sting of the fiery liquid on his mangled tongue, Bruckman's voice grew stronger; and a blaze rose in his bloodshot eyes.

"I'm going to tell you everything," he panted. "I'll live that long-- then you set the law on them--blast them off the earth! I've kept the oath until now, even with the threat of death hanging over me, but I thought I could fool them. Curse their black souls, I'll keep their secret no longer! Don't talk or ask questions--listen!"

Strange the tales that dying lips have gasped, but never a stranger tale than that Emmett Glanton heard in the blood-stained room, where a dead black face grinned by a smoldering hearth, and a dying man, spiked to a table, mouthed grisly secrets with a mangled tongue in the smoky light of the guttering lamp, while the black wind moaned and crawled at the rattling windows.

"When I was young, in another land," panted John Bruckman, "I was a fool. And I was trapped by my own folly into joining a cult of devil worshippers--the Black Brothers of Ahriman. Until too late I did not realize what they were--nor to what horrors my own terrible oath had bound me. I need not speak of their aims and purposes--they were foul beyond conception. Yet they had one characteristic that is so often lacking in many such cults--they were sincere--fanatic. They worshipped the fiend Ahriman as zealously as did their heathen ancestors. And they practiced human sacrifice. Once each year, on this very night, between midnight and dawn, a young girl was offered up on the burning altar of Ahriman, Lord of Fire. On that glowing altar her body was consumed to ashes and the ashes scattered to the night wind by the black-painted priests.

"I became one of the Black Brothers. On my breast was tattooed indelibly the symbol of Ahriman, which is the symbol of Night--a blind, black face. But at last I sickened of the revolting practices of the cult, and fled from it. I came to America and changed my name. Some of my people were already here--the branch of the family to which Joan belongs.

"With the passing of nineteen years I thought the Black Brothers had forgotten me. I didn't know there were branches in America, in the teeming foreign quarters of the great cities. But I might have known they never forget. And one day I received a cryptic message that shattered my illusions. They had remembered, had traced me, found me-- knew all about me. And, in punishment for my desertion, they had chosen my niece, Joan, for the yearly sacrifice.

"That was bad enough, but what nearly drove me mad with terror was knowledge of the custom that attends the sacrifice--since time immemorial it's been the habit of the Black Brothers to kill the man nearest the girl chosen for sacrifice--father, brother, husband--her 'master' according to their ritual. This is partly because of a dim phallic superstition, partly a practical way of eliminating an enemy, for the girl's protector would certainly seek vengeance.

"I knew I couldn't save Joan. She was marked for doom, but I might save myself by shifting responsibility for her to somebody else's shoulders. So I brought her here and married her to you."

"You swine!" whispered Glanton.

"It did me little good!" gasped Bruckman, his tortured head tossing from side to side. His eyes were glazing and a bloody froth rose to his livid lips. "They came shortly after you drove away. I was fool enough to let them in--told them I was no longer responsible for the chosen maiden. They laughed at me--tortured me. I broke away--got to the phone--but they had ordered my death, as a renegade brother. They drove away, leaving one of them here to attend to me. You can see he did his work well!"

"Where--where did they go?" Glanton spoke with dry lips, remembering the big automobile roaring northward.

"To your ranch--to get Joan--I told them where she was--before they started torturing me!"

"You fool! You're telling me this *now,*" Glanton yelled.

But John Bruckman did not hear, for, with a convulsion that spattered foam from his empurpled lips and tore one of the bloody spikes out of the wood, the life went out of him in one great cry.

Chapter IV - Crackling Blue Flame

Like a drunken man, Emmitt Glanton left from that lamp-lit room where a black face on the floor grinned blindly at a blind white face lolling on the table. The black wind ripped at him with mad, invisible fingers as he ran in great leaps to his car.

The drive through the screaming darkness was nightmare, with the black wall splitting before him, and closing behind him, horror hounding him like a werewolf on his trail, and the wind howling awful secrets in his ears.

He did not turn aside for the somber knoll this time, but plunged straight on, thundered over the bridge and rushed past the black cliff. No boulder fell from above. Joshua must have left his ambush long ago.

Three more miles and his heart leaped into his throat and stuck there, a choking chunk of ice. He should be able to see the light in the ranch house window by now--but only the glare of his own headlights knifed the black curtain before him.

Then the ranch house bulked out of the night and on the porch he saw a strange pale spot of radiance glowing. There was no sign of the automobile that had come northward. But he checked his own car suddenly to avoid running over a shape that sprawled in the fenceless yard. It was the mad Joshua, lying face down, one side of his head a mass of blood. He had come only to meet death.

Glanton slid out of the car and ran toward the house, shouting Sanchez' name. His cries died away in the stormy clamor of the wind and an icy hand gripped his heart.

His dilated eyes were fixed on the pale spot that grew in size and shape as he approached--a man's face stared at him--the face of Sanchez, weirdly illuminated. Glanton stole closer, holding his breath. Why should the face of Sanchez glow so in the darkness? Why should he stand so still, unanswering, eyes fixed and glassy? Why should his face be looking down from such a height?

Then Glanton knew. He was looking at Sanchez' severed head, fastened by its long hair to a pillar of the porch. Some sort of phosphorus had been rubbed on the dead face to make that eerie glow.

"Joan!"

It was a cry of agony as Glanton flung himself into the darkened house. Only the wind outside answered him, mocked him. His foot struck something heavy and yielding just inside the door. Sick with horror he found a match and struck it. Near the door lay a headless body, riddled with bullets. It was the body of Sanchez. And but for the corpse the house was empty. The match burned down to Glanton's fingers and he stumbled out of the house.

Out in the yard he fought down hysteria and forced himself to look at the matter rationally. Joshua must have been shot by Sanchez, while trying to sneak up on the house. Then it would have been easy for strangers to catch the old Mexican off-guard. He had not expected an attack from anyone except the halfwit, nor would he have been expecting enemies to come in a motor car. He would have come to the door at a hail from a stopping auto, unsuspectingly showing himself in the lighted doorway. A sudden hail of bullets would have done the rest. And then--beads of perspiration broke out on his body. Joan, alone and undefended, with those fiends!

He whirled, gun in hand, as he thought he heard a noise like something moving in the bushes north of the house. It diminished, ceased as he went in that direction. It might have been a steer, or some smaller beast. It might--suddenly he turned and strode toward the car.

The body that had lain there before was gone. Had dead Joshua risen and stalked away in the shadows, and was it he that Glanton had heard stealing northward through the bushes? Glanton did not greatly care. At that moment he was ready to believe any grisliness was possible, and he had no interest in Joshua, dead or alive.

He walked around the house, wiping the sweat from his face with clammy hands. The house stood on a rise. From it he could see the lights of any car fleeing northward, for several miles. He strained his eyes, but saw no distant shaft splitting the dark. The raiders must have already put many miles between them and the scene of their crimes. He must follow--but where? Northward, yes--but a few miles north of his ranch the road split into three forks, each leading eventually into a highway, one of which ran to New Mexico, one to Oklahoma, and one north into the Panhandle.

He twisted his fingers together in an agony of indecision. Then he stiffened.

He had seen a light--yet not a distinct shaft like a car light. This was more like a blur in the dark--like the glow of embers not yet extinguished. It seemed to emanate from a spot somewhat east of the road which ran north, and this side of the forks. Night made sight and judgment deceptive, but tracing out that eerie glow was better than sitting in racking inaction.

Fixing the spot in his mind as well as he could, he ran to his car and drove northward. As soon as he had descended the rise on which his house stood he could no longer see the glare, but he drove on until he reached a spot which he believed was the point where the road most closely approached the spot where he had seen the glow. A long wooded ridge stood east of the road at that spot.

He left the car and toiled up the western slope of the ridge, scratching his hands and tearing his clothing on rocks and bushes. And nearly to the crest he heard something that stopped him in his tracks. The wind had dwindled to a fitful moaning, and somewhere ahead of him there rose a weird sound that set his flesh crawling.

Chanting! Beyond that black ridge men were chanting in an evil monotone that brought up shuddersome racial memories, old as time and dim as nightmares, of grim black temples where clouds of foul incense smoke rolled about the feet of bowing worshippers before a blood-stained altar. In a frenzy Glanton charged to the crest, tearing through the thickets by sheer force.

Crouching there he looked down on a scene that wrenched his horrified mind back a thousand years into the black night of the medieval when madness stalked the earth in the guise of men.

At the foot of the ridge, in a wide, natural basin glowed a ring of fire. He saw its apparent source--boulders had been rolled to form a solid circle and these boulders glowed with a blue-white light that was like an icy heat beyond human comprehension. From them rose a glow that hung like an unholy halo above the shallow basin. It was this light he had seen from his ranch. It might have been a glow from the slag-heaps of Hell. And devils were not lacking. He saw them, three of them inside the circle--tall, muscular men, naked, black as the night that surrounded them, their heads hidden by grinning golden masks made like the faces of beasts.

They stood about a heap of stones which glowed with a dull blue radiance, and on that crude improvised altar lay a slender, white, unmoving figure.

Glanton almost screamed aloud at the sight. Joan lay there, stark naked, spread-eagled in the form of St. Andrew's Cross, her wrists and ankles strapped securely. In that instant Glanton knew what it would mean to him to lose that girl--realized how much she had come to mean to him in the few hours he had known her. His wife! Even at this moment the phrase brought a strange, warm thrill. And now those devils down there were preparing, by some hellish art, to reduce that lovely body into ashes--

Madly he hurled himself down the slope, pistol in hand. As he went he heard the chanting cease, and was aware of a strange, yet curiously familiar humming in the air.

Whence it came he could not tell, but it sounded like the pulsing of a giant dynamo. Joan cried out. An edge of pain vibrated through her voice.

The halo over the circle mounted, grew more intensely blue. The rocks glowed with a fiercer light; pale tongues of flame licked up from them. The hue of the altar under the girl was changing. The blue was growing more pronounced, less dull. That the change in its color was accompanied by painful sensations was evident from Joan's cries and the writhings of her bound body.

Glanton yelled incoherently as his feet hit level ground, and the black men turned quickly toward him. His lips drew back in a wolfish snarl and the old single-action gun went up in a menacing arc as he thumbed back the fanged hammer. He meant to shoot these devils down in their tracks, like so many mad dogs--then his out-thrust left hand touched one of the glowing boulders. Merely touched it, but the contact was like the jolt of a fork of lightning. Glanton was knocked off his feet and rolled, blind and dizzy with brief but stunning agony. As he staggered up, snarling and still gripping his gun, he recognized the truth.

Somehow those boulders had been made conductors of electricity. They were charged with a voltage terrific beyond his understanding. And so was the altar, though as yet the full force had not been turned on.

The rising hum that now filled the air told its own grisly tale. Joan was to die by electricity, not swiftly shocked to death as in an electric chair, but slowly agonizedly, burned to a crisp--to white ashes to be scattered to the night wind.

With an inhuman yell he threw up his gun and fired. One of the masked men spun on his heels and fell sprawling, but the taller of the remaining two bent quickly and laid a hand on some sort of contraption at his feet.

Instantly the hum grew to a shriek. White fire danced around the ring, blinding and dazzling the man outside. He saw the tall black forms within it vaguely, through a dizzying blue-white curtain of flame.

Shielding his eyes from the glare, panic tugging at his soul, he fired again and again until the hammer fell with an empty snap. He could not hit them. The noise, the glare, bewildered him; everything was thrown out of its proper proportions; vision and perspective were distorted.

He hurled the gun at them and reeled toward the blazing barricade with his bare hands, knowing that to touch it would be death, yet choosing death rather than standing by and watching the girl die. But before he reached it a black shape hurtled past him, out of the darkness. Joshua! Blood clotted his scalp, but his primitive fury, his mad desire for the white body on that glowing altar were undimmed.

Like a charging bull he came out of the dark, headlong at the barrier. Running hard and low he bent, gathered his thews and leaped! Only a beast or a madman could have made that leap. He cleared the barrier with a foot to spare; one instant he was etched in mid-air, black against the glare, arms wide and fingers spread like talons, then he hit catlike on his feet within the ring of death.

And as he struck he lunged. The priests were naked and weaponless. The taller let go the lever he held, sprang aside, stooped and snatched up some object, even as Joshua struck his companion. It might have been a bull that smote and tossed the black priest.

Plain above the lessening hum and crackle of blue flame sounded the snap of splintering bones, the shriek of the priest. He was whirled from his feet, a broken, dangling doll, lifted high in apelike arms above the bullet-head and dashed head first to the earth with such fury that the broken corpse rebounded before it lay still. Head down, the killer plunged at the taller priest's throat.

It had been a pistol this man had snatched up, and a raking blast of lead met the charging madman--met him, but did not stop him.

With bullets smacking into his body at close range, Joshua bellowed with pain and swayed on his feet, but came on in an irresistible surge of fury and threw his arms about the black body of his foe. He must have been dying even then, but the blind force of his rush was enough to carry the priest off his feet. Together they hurtled on--to crash full against the blazing ring of boulders!

A crack like a clap of thunder, a blinding spray of blue fire, one awful scream--then the reek of burnt flesh filled the air. In the swiftly dying glare, Emmett Glanton saw two hideous figures--*both* black now--crumpled in a fused, indistinguishable mass against the dulling rocks.

Something had happened to the generator of that terrible power. The hum had ceased; the demon halo was dying. Already the stones of the altar had assumed their natural tint. But on it the girl lay limp.

As Glanton crawled over the barrier his heart was in his mouth. Tenderly he freed her and lifted her, grateful to feel warm, living flesh under his hands, but setting his teeth against what he might find--but her tender back and limbs showed none of the ghastly burns he feared.

Obviously no great amount of electricity had been turned into the altar. He saw wires running in all directions from the amazingly small, compact, black case-like thing that stood near the altar.

Before he carried Joan out of the ring he smashed the thing with a heavy rock. The Black Brothers knew secrets that were better kept from the world at large. Even clean science became hurtful black magic in their hands. That tiny dynamo, of a type undreamed of by the world, contained more energy than sane men conceived of--power to turn naked rocks into live wires. Such a secret could only be evil.

He whipped off his torn shirt and wrapped the girl in it, as carefully he carried her down to the road.

As he went, he thought of Joshua, and the only logical explanation offered itself. The bullet that had struck the madman had not killed him, but only creased him and knocked him out. When he came to himself, he started on the trail of the woman his crazed brain desired, drawn either by the same glimpse of the distant fire that had drawn Glanton, or by dark, psychic instinct.

Glanton had almost reached the car when Joan opened her eyes, stared about her wildly, then clung to him.

"It's all right, kid," he soothed her. "You're not hurt. You just fainted. Everything's all right now. Joshua paid his debt, without meaning to, poor devil. Look, it's getting daylight. The night's past."

He meant it in more than its literal sense. "Take me home, Emmett," she whimpered, nestling deep into his arms. Then, irrelevantly: "Kiss me."

And Emmett Glanton kissed his wife for the first time, just as dawn touched the eastern hills.

171

Also from Benediction Books …
Wandering Between Two Worlds: Essays on Faith and Art
Anita Mathias
Benediction Books, 2007
152 pages
ISBN: 0955373700

Available from www.amazon.com, www.amazon.co.uk

In these wide-ranging lyrical essays, Anita Mathias writes, in lush, lovely prose, of her naughty Catholic childhood in Jamshedpur, India; her large, eccentric family in Mangalore, a sea-coast town converted by the Portuguese in the sixteenth century; her rebellion and atheism as a teenager in her Himalayan boarding school, run by German missionary nuns, St. Mary's Convent, Nainital; and her abrupt religious conversion after which she entered Mother Teresa's convent in Calcutta as a novice. Later rich, elegant essays explore the dualities of her life as a writer, mother, and Christian in the United States-- Domesticity and Art, Writing and Prayer, and the experience of being "an alien and stranger" as an immigrant in America, sensing the need for roots.

About the Author

Anita Mathias is the author of *Wandering Between Two Worlds: Essays on Faith and Art.* She has a B.A. and M.A. in English from Somerville College, Oxford University, and an M.A. in Creative Writing from the Ohio State University, USA. Anita won a National Endowment of the Arts fellowship in Creative Nonfiction in 1997. She lives in Oxford, England with her husband, Roy, and her daughters, Zoe and Irene.

Anita's website:
  http://www.anitamathias.com, and
Anita's blog Dreaming Beneath the Spires:
  http://dreamingbeneaththespires.blogspot.com

The Church That Had Too Much
Anita Mathias
Benediction Books, 2010
52 pages
ISBN: 9781849026567

Available from www.amazon.com, www.amazon.co.uk

The Church That Had Too Much was very well-intentioned. She
wanted to love God, she wanted to love people, but she was both ham-
pered by her muchness and the abundance of her possessions, and
beset by ambition, power struggles and snobbery. Read about the sur-
prising way The Church That Had Too Much began to resolve her
problems in this deceptively simple and enchanting fable.

About the Author

Anita Mathias is the author of *Wandering Between Two Worlds: Essays on Faith and Art*. She has a B.A. and M.A. in English from
Somerville College, Oxford University, and an M.A. in Creative Writing from the Ohio State University, USA. Anita won a National
Endowment of the Arts fellowship in Creative Nonfiction in 1997.
She lives in Oxford, England with her husband, Roy, and her daughters, Zoe and Irene.

Anita's website:
    http://www.anitamathias.com, and
Anita's blog Dreaming Beneath the Spires:
    http://dreamingbeneaththespires.blogspot.com

Collected Ghost Stories
M R James
Benediction Books, 2011
284 pages
ISBN: 978-1-84902-454-9

Available from www.amazon.com, www.amazon.co.uk

Collected Ghost Stories by M R James is a collection of twenty-two
ghost stories, plus a fascinating essay on the writing of ghost stories.
Montague Rhodes James (1862–1936) was a medieval scholar and
Provost of King's College, Cambridge. His stories are classics of their
genre, understated, beautifully paced and almost never explicit. Their
idyllic rural backgrounds and amiable hero make the chilling terror of
otherworldly intrusions all the more horrific.

The Uncommon Prayer-Book;
A Neighbour's Landmark;
Rats;
The Experiment;
The Malice Of Inanimate Objects;
A Vignette;
Canon Alberic's Scrap-Book;
The Stalls Of Barchester Cathedral;
An Episode Of Cathedral History;
The Story Of A Disappearance And An Appearance;
The Haunted Dolls' House;
Lost Hearts;
Mr. Humphreys And His Inheritance;
Martin's Close;
The Diary Of Mr. Poynter;
The Rose-Garden;
Casting The Runes;
A School Story;
The Tractate Middoth;
Two Doctors;
A View From A Hill;
The Residence At Whitminster;
Appendix: M. R. James On Ghost Stories

Note: This is not to be confused with the Book "The Collected Ghost
Stories of M R James" which was published in 1931.

Collected Twilight Stories
Marjorie Bowen
Benediction Books, 2011
266 pages
ISBN: 978-1-84902-453-2

Available from www.amazon.com, www.amazon.co.uk

'Collected Twilight Stories' is a compilation of eighteen of Marjorie Bowen's supernatural horror stories. 'Marjorie Bowen' is a nom de plume of the British Author Gabrielle Margaret Vere Long (1885-1952). Sally Benson in The New Yorker (1965) describes her work under the pseudonym 'Joseph Shearing' - "[she] is a painstaking researcher, a superb writer, a careful technician, and a master of horror. There is no one else quite like [her]". Gabrielle's father was an alchoholic and he left the family home when she was young, eventually being found dead on a London street. Consequently, her writings were the main source of income for her family. She was married twice, initially for four years to a Sicilian named Zefferino Emilio Constanza, who died of turberculosis, and then to Arthur L. Long. This collection comprises the following eighteen short stories:

Scoured Silk;
The Breakdown;
One Remained Behind - A Romance A La Mode Gothique;
The House By The Poppy Field;
Half-Past Two;
Elsie's Lonely Afternoon;
The Extraordinary Adventure Of Mr John Proudie;
Ann Mellor's Lover;
Florence Flannery;
Kecksies;
The Avenging Of Ann Leete;
The Bishop Of Hell;
The Crown Derby Plate;
The Fair Hair Of Ambrosine;
The Housekeeper;
Raw Material;
The Hidden Ape;
The Sign-Painter And The Crystal Fishes